A SENTIMENTAL JOURNEY

Laurence Sterne was born in 1713 at Clonmel in Ireland, the son of an army ensign. From 1723 until his father's death in 1731 he was sent to school in Halifax, Yorkshire, and in 1733 he entered as a sizar at Jesus College, Cambridge, receiving his B.A. in 1737. With the help of his uncle Jacques, precentor and canon of York, Sterne earned his livings. He took holy orders and in 1738 obtained the living of Sutton-in-the-Forest, near York, and a prebend in the cathedral. In 1741 he married, and through his wife's influence received the neighbouring benefice of Stillington. Their marriage was generally unhappy. Sterne's literary career began late; his first publication, a pamphlet called *A Political Romance*, appeared in 1759. In the same year he began his masterpiece, *The Life and Opinions of Tristram Shandy*. The first two volumes made him a celebrity and he visited London where he was lavishly fêted. Between 1761 and 1767 he brought out a further seven volumes. Sterne was dogged by ill-health for much of his life and during his latter years he alternated bouts of being lionized in London with recuperative continental travels. *A Sentimental Journey*, published in 1768, was created from a seven-month trip through France and Italy. Laurence Sterne died in London in 1768.

Laurence Sterne

A SENTIMENTAL JOURNEY
THROUGH
FRANCE AND ITALY

EDITED BY
GRAHAM PETRIE
WITH AN INTRODUCTION
BY A. ALVAREZ

PENGUIN BOOKS

PENGUIN BOOKS

Published by the Penguin Group
27 Wrights Lane, London W8 5TZ, England
Viking Penguin Inc., 40 West 23rd Street, New York, New York 10010, USA
Penguin Books Australia Ltd, Ringwood, Victoria, Australia
Penguin Books Canada Ltd, 2801 John Street, Markham, Ontario, Canada L3R 1B4
Penguin Books (NZ) Ltd, 182–190 Wairau Road, Auckland 10, New Zealand

Penguin Books Ltd, Registered Offices: Harmondsworth, Middlesex, England

First published 1768
Published in the Penguin English Library, 1967
Reprinted in Penguin Classics 1986
5 7 9 10 8 6 4

Introduction copyright © A. Alvarez, 1967
(a version of this introduction was published in the *Hudson Review*
Vol. XIX No. 4, Winter 1966–7)
Notes copyright © Graham Petrie, 1967
All rigths reserved

Made and printed in Great Britain by
BPCC Hazell Books
Aylesbury, Bucks, England
Member of BPCC Ltd.
Set in Linotype Georgian

CONTENTS

INTRODUCTION

'Le moral, c'est le travelling'
– Jean-Luc Godard

LAURENCE STERNE is a distinctly 'modern' novelist. He has the freedom, the total originality, the sense of a man creating the form from scratch and for himself, that we now expect of any serious artist. He has, too, the modernist's apparent indifference to rules, as though aesthetic formalities were, in the final analysis, boring, and the only vindication of a work of art were the immediacy with which it expresses the personality of its creator. Casualness, in short, was his declared artistic principle:

... of all the several ways of beginning a book which are now in practice throughout the known world, I am confident my own way of doing it is the best – I'm sure it is the most religious – for I begin with writing the first sentence – and trusting to Almighty God for the second. [*Tristram Shandy*, VIII, 2.]

Obviously, he wasn't anything like as haphazard as he wished to appear. We know from his manuscripts that he wrote and meticulously rewrote, crowding the margins with changes and alternatives, in order to give his prose precisely that casual, dashed-off air, the surface flicker of a sensibility in motion.* Yet the effect he achieved with all his effort was of a fined-down disregard for art.

He was also the first modernist in the way in which he cut the novel clear from the constrictions of traditional narrative, setting it free into the realm of personality, into almost a kind of proto-expressionism. Granted, he took his method largely from the picaresque novel; his masters were Rabelais and Cervantes. Yet the picaresque is essentially the

*See *The Life and Times of Laurence Sterne* by Wilbur I. Cross, New Haven, third edition, 1929, pp. 471–7.

form for obsessional story-tellers: one tale leads compulsively to another, as though the fate of the narrator of the *Arabian Nights* hung over every picaresque author's head. In comparison, Sterne seems not much interested in stories. Occasionally he digresses into narrative, but mostly he simply digresses, as yet another fascinating and seemingly urgent side-issue crosses his mind. And these digressions, like his two novels themselves, are substantially without plots. The whole rickety substance is supported and validated simply by the flow of talk, talk, talk. It reads like a picaresque novel transformed into abstract art.

There is a belief, which Sterne himself encouraged, that he learned this method from John Locke and his theory of the association of ideas.* It seems to me equally possible that it was merely part of his Irish inheritance. Though his father, Ensign Roger Sterne, was English – an amiable Army failure descended from a long line of tough and successful Yorkshire churchmen – his mother had Irish connexions. (She, too, was an apparent disaster: a nagging wife and an indifferent, rapacious mother, she was the stepdaughter of a camp sutler to whom Roger Sterne owed money.) Laurence himself was born in Dublin and spent the early part of his childhood billeted on occasional Irish relatives. Although most of his schooldays and the rest of his life were spent in Yorkshire – with intermittent forays on London and the continent – his work is controlled by that compulsive talkativeness you find undiluted only in an Irish barroom virtuoso. And he recreated the novel in that image, evolving a style of pure talk, of controlled inconsequentiality, irrelevance and continual interruption. This was a form both new and not immediately usable. So, although his influence was enormous in his day, it bypassed the nineteenth century, when the novel became more settled and staid in its ways. His lineal descendants are the heroes of Samuel Beckett's fiction, with their endless 'quaqua'.

* See *Tristram Shandy's World* by John Traugott, Berkeley, 1954.

Given this lack of plot or even moral purpose, either improving or scurrilous, you are left for connexions and artistic control simply with a personal tone of voice, the flow of casual, intimate, highly idiosyncratic conversation. Even *Tristram Shandy*'s extraordinary gallery of eccentrics – Uncle Toby, My Father, My Mother, Trim, Dr Slop, Yorick, the Widow Wadman – have very little substance of their own; they rely on the author's amused, vague tenderness to make sense of their lives. They are less characters in their own right than obsessions held together by his indulgence.

This is still more marked in *A Sentimental Journey*, where the people are described hardly at all. It is perhaps the most bodiless novel ever written. Though incident is piled on incident, none really amounts to much, and the book relies for its effect entirely on Sterne's ability to buttonhole his readers. For that he had an unprecedented genius. He was master of some curious sleight of tone which sucks you at once into the most intimate and private workings of his mind. He had, as another Irishman, W. B. Yeats, said of a third, George Moore, 'the terrible gift of intimacy'.

Maybe this gift was so unfalteringly his throughout his literary career because he began so late and was spared a hesitant apprenticeship. His first effort, a pamphlet called *A Political Romance*, was not published until the beginning of 1759, when he was already in his mid-forties; *Tristram Shandy* began to appear at the end of the same year. By the time he came to *A Sentimental Journey*, nine years later, his intimacy with the audience was instinctive and assured. Indeed, the novel is elaborately that of a famous man. Sterne writes as though from a certain height of success; he is knowingly a public personality, a fashionable figure on the literary landscape, confident and rather delighted by the exposure. The incident with the Count de B**** – who suddenly realizes that the shabby charmer who is begging his help in obtaining a passport is in fact a famous author – and the description of how he rode the circuit of

9

smart Parisian parties are done with the evident relish of a man who enjoyed his fame.

Yet clearly something more is involved than naïve pleasure in his success and his distance from his Yorkshire parsonage and half-mad wife. By 1768, Sterne's fame, his novels and his personality were, to an unusual degree, all of a piece. He had wholly entered the Shandean world he himself had created. The first-person narrator is himself a character from the earlier novel: he is Yorick, parson and friend of the Shandys, whom Sterne had prematurely killed off in the first volume – mourning his decease with two pages of solid black – and then resurrected whenever convenient, thanks to a time-scheme which leaps years between lines and extends seconds through whole paragraphs. Granted, the personalities of Sterne and Yorick were inextricably entwined well before the final novel: Sterne called himself Yorick in his letters and even published his sermons under that name. But by the time he came to *A Sentimental Journey* the name was something more than a semi-private joke to draw the initiated reader into the author's elite circle. Instead, it seemed to sum up a whole nexus of Sterne's preoccupations: with wit and melancholy and death. Yorick the jester was also Yorick the death's head, and Sterne, who had spat blood with increasing seriousness since his undergraduate days at Cambridge, was knowingly a dying man when he began the *Journey*. So perhaps it gave him a soothing illusion of immortality to identify so completely with a character in his own work; more probably, it allowed enough free air to circulate between himself and his situation, so that his wit had space in which to manoeuvre.

There were also certain practical advantages. In part, Sterne wrote this last novel to clear, or at least to redefine, his name. As a writer his reputation was, by then, vast and international, but as a parson it had suffered correspondingly. His difficulty was that, like most compulsive talkers, he could never resist the jokey, bawdy possibilities of whatever turned up along the way in his monologues. His fellow clerics objected accordingly: his work was altogether too smutty, too obsessed, too unseemly for a man of the church. So one purpose of *A Sentimental Journey* was to prove his innocence. His letters at the time ring with the theme. He wrote to his daughter that the design of the book was 'to teach us to love the world and our fellow creatures better than we do – so it runs most upon those gentle passions and affections, which aid so much to it'. To another, slightly older, young woman it was the same story:

... I have something else for you, which I am fabricating at a great rate, and that is my Journey, which shall make you cry as much as ever it made me laugh – or I'll give up the Business of sentimental writing – and write to the Body.

It was even the same to his diplomat friend, Sir George Macartney, though the tone was a little cooler: 'I shall', he wrote, 'have the honour of presenting to you a couple of as clean brats as ever chaste brain conceived'.

Sterne had always written from his nerve-ends, with a quivering, edgy liveliness; the new novel was to show that this was genuinely the product of an intensity of emotion, not of mere nerviness. On the surface, there was something almost didactic in its purpose: it would teach people how to react, show them that the simplest incident – an innocent exchange with a mendicant monk, a peasant with his dead donkey – swarmed with high feeling. It would show them that the value of travelling was not in stunning adventures or strenuous sightseeing or exquisite views exquisitely rendered back into prose; it was, instead, in the traveller's receptiveness to feelings, and the flair and subtlety with which he expressed them.

Admittedly, Sterne was cashing in on a fad. Almost twenty years before, a Lady Bradshage had written querulously to Richardson:

What, in your opinion, is the meaning of the word *sentimental*, so much in vogue among the polite ... Everything clever and agreeable is comprehended in that word ... I am frequently astonished to hear such a one is a *sentimental* man; we were a *sentimental* party; I have been taking a *sentimental* walk ...

Sterne took this London fad and made it into an international obsession. The word was adopted into French and German because of his novel. There were circles of Sterne addicts in Germany who studied the master, cultivated exquisite feelings and, after the manner of Yorick and the friar, presented each other with little horn snuff-boxes, promising, according to Professor Cross, 'to cultivate Yorick's gentleness, content with fortune, and pity and pardon for all human errors'. No doubt it was excessive; certainly, all this stood Sterne in peculiarly bad stead with the Victorians: he was credited with all the morbid sensibility and snobbish high feeling they loathed. In *The English Humourists* Thackeray attacked him as a supreme hypocrite, flailing him for his combination of sentimentality and prurience.

To be disliked by Thackeray is, admittedly, a fair recommendation. Even so, Sterne has never quite escaped the charge of playing up his sensitivity. Even his defenders imply that he overdid things and, in his concern not to appear bawdy, went too far the other way, ending as a dandified tear-jerker. This seems to me to disregard the whole strategy of the novel: every exquisite moment is promptly undercut either by irony or by deliberate absurdity. Consider, for example, the much abused episode of the peasant lamenting his dead donkey. It was a kind of eighteenth-century death of Little Nell, energetically wept over at the time and strenuously savaged later. Neither the admirers nor the detractors seem to have got the point. Sterne ends the passage by drawing the inevitable moral:

Shame on the world! said I to myself – Did we love each other, as this poor soul but loved his ass – 'twould be something. —

The next chapter begins immediately:

> The concern which the poor fellow's story threw me into, required some attention; the postillion paid not the least to it, but set off upon the *pavé* in a full gallop.
>
> The thirstiest soul in the most sandy desert of Arabia could not have wished more for a cup of cold water, than mine did for grave and quiet movements; and I should have had a high opinion of the postillion, had he but stolen off with me in something like a pensive pace. — On the contrary, as the mourner finished his lamentation, the fellow gave an unfeeling lash to each of his beasts, and set off clattering like a thousand devils.

So instead of being able to lie back and soak in his feelings, Yorick is promptly embroiled in a shouting match with the postillion. Only when his nerves are so thoroughly jangled that he needs the release of a hard gallop does the coachman slow to a walking pace. The whole thing is a paradigm of frustration, and a joke at his own expense.

This, I think, is the rule for the novel, not the exception. The more elegantly sentimental the narrator's responses, the more absurd the after-effects. It is Sterne's particular strength as a comic writer that no matter how whole-heartedly he pursues high feeling, unredeemed reality keeps breaking in. So whatever the immediate propagandist issues for his contemporaries – for or against the sentimental education – it seems to me now to be genuinely impossible to read him as anything except a supreme, and supremely consistent, ironist.

Perhaps that is the least that can be expected of an eighteenth-century wit. Yet Sterne's irony, like most other elements of his writing, has a distinctly modern taste to it. The incident with the beautiful Grisset, for example. Yorick, strolling in Paris, is more or less lost; 'more or less' since he doesn't bother to ask the way until he can find someone attractive enough to be worth asking. Finally, he sees the beautiful Grisset working in her shop; together they go through an elaborate ritual of question and answer, she giving him directions, he repeating them to her, she repeating them back to him; he leaves, forgets the directions in a few paces, and returns; at length they settle down to an intimate tête-à-tête in her shop. It is like the mating dance of two tropical birds. Finally, by the way of elegant compliment, he takes her wrist and feels her pulse:

I had counted twenty pulsations, and was going on fast towards the fortieth, when her husband coming unexpectedly from the back parlour into the shop, put me a little out in my reckoning. — 'Twas nobody but her husband, she said – so I began a fresh score — Monsieur is so good, quoth she, as he passed us by, as to give himself the trouble of feeling my pulse — The husband took off his hat, and making me a bow, said, I did him too much honour – and having said that, he put on his hat and walked out.

The beautifully poised and pausing rhythm of the prose, by which Sterne passes off an outrageous situation as though it were utterly normal, is the essence of his art. It is also the essence of the modern 'cool' style, the art of controlled and detached delinquency. Yet this is not a quality which has yet been expressed with any great subtlety in prose. And this is the crux of the matter when calling Sterne a modernist: if there is a close contemporary equivalent to his work it is not to be found in any novelist; it is, instead, in the films of the French director, Jean-Luc Godard.

What Sterne and Godard have in common is a style and an obsession, or rather, a style to cope with an obsession. By style I mean something beyond their elegance and wit and detachment. Instead, it is the ability to maintain all those qualities whilst not leaving anything out, whilst refusing a narrow, exclusive focus. The novelist's sensibility and the director's camera are so alive, so eclectic, that when they move down a street the whole casual scene is drawn into the action:

I walked up gravely to the window in my dusty black coat, and looking through the glass saw all the world in yellow, blue, and green, running at the ring of pleasure.

And the action itself is casual. The plot in Godard's movies may be marginally tighter than in Sterne's novels, but it is rarely more important. What matters are the incidents that proliferate along the route, and the way in which they are handled.

Hence casualness and unprejudiced receptivity become an artistic procedure. And this, in a way, is a delinquent aesthetic: the artist creates a work at the same time as he comments, implicitly but nihilistically, on the art-form and the whole choosy business of art. Neither Sterne nor Godard seems to believe in anything beyond what is there, present to the senses, at the moment. Questioned by a pompous interviewer on the morality of his films, Godard replied, 'Le moral, c'est le travelling'. He was implying, to say the least, that morality is strictly empirical, since 'le travelling' is a technical film-maker's term to describe the movement of the camera; morality, that is, is to be picked up and discarded again, as you go along. Sterne has precisely the same unrehearsed attitude to what occurs. So both are delinquent to the extent of, first, being unconcerned with any preordained moral order and, second, in their seemingly delighted assumption that, beneath all the elegance, their protagonists are interested only in gratifying their momentary impulses – though without unnecessary viciousness; the wit of both is essentially gentle. In their worlds everyone, elegantly, sadly, in one way or another, is on the make.

This, I think, is the basic assumption behind all Sterne's ambiguities. For example, the intense, finger-tip flirtation between Yorick and Madame de R****'s 'fair *fille de chambre*' in the chapter called 'The Temptation'. The narrator returns to his hotel to find her waiting; in that curious, typical, slow-motion narrative, where every slight gesture can endure for whole lines, he takes her back up to his room and then, little by little, leads her from the desk, to the door, to the bed, where they sit exchanging quivering civilities:

A strap had given way in her walk, and the buckle of her shoe was just falling off – See, said the *fille de chambre*, holding up her foot — I could not for my soul but fasten the buckle in return, and putting in the strap – and lifting up the other foot with it, when I had done, to see both were right – in doing it too suddenly – it unavoidably threw the fair *fille de chambre* off her center – and then ——

THE CONQUEST

YES — and then — Ye whose clay-cold heads and lukewarm hearts can argue down or mask your passions, tell me, what trespass is it that man should have them? or how his spirit stands answerable to the father of spirits, but for his conduct under them?

If nature has so wove her web of kindness, that some threads of love and desire are entangled with the piece, must the whole web be rent in drawing them out? — Whip me such stoics, great governor of nature! said I to myself — Wherever thy providence shall place me for the trials of my virtue – whatever is my danger – whatever is my situation – *let me feel the movements which rise out of it, and which belong to me as a man, and if I govern them as a good one, I will trust the issues to thy justice* — for thou hast made us, and not we ourselves.

As I finished my address, I raised the fair *fille de chambre* up by the hand, and led her out of the room — she stood by me till I locked the door and put the key in my pocket – *and then* – the victory being quite decisive – and not till then, I pressed my lips to her cheek, and, taking her by the hand again, led her safe to the gate of the hotel.

This is *double entendre* raised to high art. The lines I have italicized could as easily describe the act of making love as the reasons for abstaining from it. So who is conquered in 'The Conquest': Yorick or 'the fair *fille de chambre*'? Sterne avers that it is the former, but the whole passage seems to point the other way.

It was presumably this kind of moral punning that Coleridge objected to in his *Literary Remains*:

With regard to Sterne, and the charge of licentiousness which presses so seriously upon his character as a writer, I would remark that there is a sort of knowingness, the wit of which depends, 1st, on the modesty it gives pain to; or, 2ndly, on the innocence and innocent ignorance over which it triumphs; or, 3rdly, on a certain oscillation in the individual's own mind between the remaining good and the encroaching evil of his nature – a sort of dallying with the devil – a fluxionary art of combining courage and cowardice, as when a man snuffs a candle with his fingers for the first time, or better still, perhaps, like that trembling daring with which a child touches a hot tea-urn, because it has been forbidden; so that the mind has its own white and black angel.... We have only to suppose a society innocent, and then nine-tenths of this sort of wit would be like a stone that falls in snow, making no sound, because exciting no resistance; the remainder rests on its being an offence against the good manners of human nature itself.

To some extent this is justified, but only by virtue of mis-reading the tone of the man. Sterne seems to snigger only if read with the bias of nineteenth-century moral solidity and assurance. Judged by the more improvised standards he seems to have shared with the mid twentieth century, the nastiness disappears entirely. The joke is there for those who can see it, but is not insistent enough to offend those who can't. Either way, it remains a joke; the criterion is enjoyment; the author demands simply that the reader relish as much as he does the full, ambiguous subtlety of the situation, with no moral *parti pris*.

Yet Sterne, again like Godard, is not as cool as he would appear. Perhaps complete coolness is impossible for any-one except saints and certifiable schizophrenics. Elsewhere, it is more usually what William Empson once called 'a style from a despair'; under it runs a continual, plangent note of obsession. Thus Godard is obsessed with a girl – embodied usually by the beautiful Anna Karina – baffling, ungettable, promiscuous but frigid, narcissistic, rejecting, and yet, with her queer honesty, always a bit pathetic, almost innocent, certainly lost. The camera becomes an instrument of his obsession, as though he were trying with it to catch something of her elusiveness and fix it on film for keeps. Sterne, by his own confession, also thought of himself as a man obsessed by women, a perpetually pining lover. It seems to me to be nearer the truth to say that he was obsessed by feeling itself. Hence that extraordinarily consistent air of suspended eroticism which runs through most of *A Sentimental Journey*, a continual, quivering, aroused nervousness. Granted, he was constantly undercutting it, as I suggested earlier; so it became an irritant instead of a destroyer of wit. Yet there is a curious rawness about his sensibility: he is so quick and aware and brimming with responses that he writes as though he had one skin too few.

That is natural enough, considering the circumstances under which he wrote this last book. He was in the final months of his life, knowingly dying of consumption, racked by the after-effects of a savage cure for venereal disease, and desperate at the loss of a woman with whom he was – or imagined himself to be – violently in love. Mercifully, none of this gets into the *Journey*. Instead, it is chronicled at length in his *Journal to Eliza*, which was written literally in tandem with the novel. The *Journal* was never intended for publication; he kept it solely for the benefit of his latest passion, a Mrs Elizabeth Draper, who had unwillingly left him to return to her elderly husband in India. He planned to give it to her when they were reunited to show how painfully he had endured her absence. So to say that it is a terrible production – indulgent, self-pitying, hysterical – is beside the point. Yet by the tiresome excess itself, the *Journal* somehow validates the *Journey*. For it helps to define a quality in the wit which is otherwise hard to pin down. I mean one's persistent sense that the wit, for all its cool, is romantic; it is based on an illusion, even an idealism of feeling. But it is redeemed from common sentimentality because the artist is so quick and subtle and perceptive that he sees through the illusions long before the reader. Indeed, the illusions are a force impelling him into wit. So he undercuts them before anyone else has the chance.

This precarious poise is difficult to maintain at the best of times. And all the evidence seems to show that *A Sentimental Journey* was, in fact, written at the worst of times, with illness, heartbreak and death all crowding in one on another – not to mention the unexpected return of his nagging wife, which prematurely put a stop to the *Journal*. Yet it was through this private record that he managed to draw off the excess of feeling – that emotional rawness which consumptives are particularly prey to – leaving himself free to mock himself in his real art, leaving his urban, and supremely urbane, irony in complete mocking control. This is why *A Sentimental Journey* was finally not quite the spotless and improving novel he threatened in his sickness and depression. The witty, sharp-edged, casual monologue, perceptive almost to the point of over-breeding, and so cool that it begins with a casual remark and ends in the middle of a sentence in the middle of a bawdy story, was an infinitely more difficult work of art to achieve.

A. ALVAREZ

SUGGESTED FURTHER READING

Wilbur L. Cross, *The Life and Times of Laurence Sterne*, New Haven, third edition, 1929.

Ernest N. Dilworth, *The Unsentimental Journey of Laurence Sterne*, New York, 1948.

Henri Fluchère, *Laurence Sterne: From Tristram to Yorick*, English translation, London, 1965.

Gardner D. Stout, Jr, 'Yorick's Sentimental Journey: A Comic *Pilgrim's Progress* for the Man of Feeling', *English Literary History*, Vol. XXX (1963), pp. 395–412.

W. B. C. Watkins, *Perilous Balance: The Tragic Genius of Swift, Johnson, and Sterne*, London, 1939.

Virginia Woolf, Introduction to the World's Classics edition of *A Sentimental Journey*, Oxford, 1928.

A NOTE ON THE TEXT

THE text is that of the first edition of *A Sentimental Journey*, published in 1768, with the following exceptions:

1. Some obvious errors have been silently corrected.

2. Sterne's spelling has been retained, except that: (*a*) the 'long *s*' has been changed to '*s*'; (*b*) elliptical spellings, especially '—'*d*' for '—*ed*', have been expanded; (*c*) where Sterne uses both the modern and the eighteenth-century spellings of a word, the modern version has been adopted throughout.

3. Sterne's punctuation has been retained, except in a few cases where it is likely to cause difficulty to the modern reader.

4. Sterne's spelling of French words has occasionally been corrected where it is likely to cause difficulty to the modern reader. In addition, I have distinguished more consistently than Sterne himself does between the French *hôtel*, meaning a private residence, and the English *hotel*, meaning an inn.

5. The use of italics and capital letters has been rationalized to some extent, and titles of books have been italicized throughout.

All footnotes in the text are Sterne's.

GRAHAM PETRIE

Facsimile of the title page of Volume I of the first edition (1768)

A

SENTIMENTAL JOURNEY

THROUGH

FRANCE AND ITALY.

BY

Mr. YORICK.

VOL. I.

LONDON:

Printed for T. BECKET and P. A. DE HONDT,
in the Strand. MDCCLXVIII.

A

SENTIMENTAL JOURNEY

THROUGH

FRANCE and ITALY

BY

Mr. YORICK

A SENTIMENTAL JOURNEY
&c. &c.

– They order, said I, this matter better in France –

– You have been in France? said my gentleman, turning quick upon me with the most civil triumph in the world. – Strange! quoth I, debating the matter with myself, That one and twenty miles sailing, for 'tis absolutely no further from Dover to Calais, should give a man these rights – I'll look into them: so giving up the argument – I went straight to my lodgings, put up half a dozen shirts and a black pair of silk breeches – 'the coat I have on, said I, looking at the sleeve, will do' – took a place in the Dover stage; and the packet sailing at nine the next morning – by three I had got sat down to my dinner upon a fricasee'd chicken, so incontestably in France, that had I died that night of an indigestion, the whole world could not have suspended the effects of the *Droits d'aubaine** – my shirts, and black pair of silk breeches – portmanteau and all must have gone to the king of France – even the little picture which I have so long worn, and so often have told thee, Eliza,[1] I would carry with me into my grave, would have been torn from my neck. – Ungenerous! – to seize upon the wreck of an unwary passenger, whom your subjects had beckoned to their coast – by heaven! Sire, it is not well done; and much does it grieve me, 'tis the monarch of a people so civilized and courteous, and so renowned for sentiment and fine feelings, that I have to reason with ——

But I have scarce set foot in your dominions —

* All the effects of strangers (Swiss and Scotch excepted) dying in France, are seized by virtue of this law, though the heir be upon the spot — the profit of these contingencies being farmed, there is no redress.

CALAIS

WHEN I had finished my dinner, and drank the king of France's health, to satisfy my mind that I bore him no spleen, but, on the contrary, high honour for the humanity of his temper – I rose up an inch taller for the accommodation.

– No – said I – the Bourbon is by no means a cruel race: they may be misled like other people; but there is a mildness in their blood. As I acknowledged this, I felt a suffusion of a finer kind, upon my cheek – more warm and friendly to man, than what Burgundy (at least of two livres a bottle, which was such as I had been drinking) could have produced.

– Just God! said I, kicking my portmanteau aside, what is there in this world's goods which should sharpen our spirits, and make so many kind-hearted brethren of us, fall out so cruelly as we do by the way?

When man is at peace with man, how much lighter than a feather is the heaviest of metals in his hand! he pulls out his purse, and holding it airily and uncompressed, looks round him, as if he sought for an object to share it with. – In doing this, I felt every vessel in my frame dilate – the arteries beat all chearily together, and every power which sustained life, performed it with so little friction, that 'twould have confounded the most *physical precieuse*[2] in France: with all her materialism, she could scarce have called me a machine –

I'm confident, said I to myself, I should have overset her creed.

The accession of that idea, carried nature, at that time, as high as she could go – I was at peace with the world before, and this finished the treaty with myself –

– Now, was I a king of France, cried I – what a moment for an orphan to have begged his father's portmanteau of me!

THE MONK

CALAIS

I HAD scarce uttered the words, when a poor monk of the order of St Francis came into the room to beg something for his convent. No man cares to have his virtues the sport of contingencies – or one man may be generous, as another man is puissant – *sed non quo ad hanc* – or be it as it may – for there is no regular reasoning upon the ebbs and flows of our humours; they may depend upon the same causes, for aught I know, which influence the tides themselves – 'twould oft be no discredit to us to suppose it was so: I'm sure at least for myself, that in many a case I should be more highly satisfied, to have it said by the world, 'I had had an affair with the moon, in which there was neither sin nor shame,' than have it pass altogether as my own act and deed, wherein there was so much of both.

– But be this as it may. The moment I cast my eyes upon him, I was predetermined not to give him a single sous; and accordingly I put my purse into my pocket – buttoned it up – set myself a little more upon my centre, and advanced up gravely to him: there was something, I fear, forbidding in my look: I have his figure this moment before my eyes, and think there was that in it which deserved better.

The monk, as I judged from the break in his tonsure, a few scattered white hairs upon his temples, being all that remained of it, might be about seventy – but from his eyes, and that sort of fire which was in them, which seemed more tempered by courtesy than years, could be no more than sixty – Truth might lie between – He was certainly sixty-five; and the general air of his countenance, notwithstanding something seemed to have been planting wrinkles in it before their time, agreed to the account.

It was one of those heads, which Guido[3] has often painted – mild, pale – penetrating, free from all commonplace

29

ideas of fat contented ignorance looking downwards upon the earth – it looked forwards; but looked, as if it looked at something beyond this world. How one of his order came by it, heaven above, who let it fall upon a monk's shoulders, best knows: but it would have suited a Bramin, and had I met it upon the plains of Indostan, I had reverenced it.

The rest of his outline may be given in a few strokes; one might put it into the hands of any one to design, for 'twas neither elegant or otherwise, but as character and expression made it so: it was a thin, spare form, something above the common size, if it lost not the distinction by a bend forwards in the figure – but it was the attitude of Entreaty; and as it now stands presented to my imagination, it gained more than it lost by it.

When he had entered the room three paces, he stood still; and laying his left hand upon his breast, (a slender white staff with which he journeyed being in his right) – when I had got close up to him, he introduced himself with the little story of the wants of his convent, and the poverty of his order – and did it with so simple a grace – and such an air of deprecation was there in the whole cast of his look and figure – I was bewitched not to have been struck with it –

– A better reason was, I had predetermined not to give him a single sous.

THE MONK

CALAIS

– 'Tis very true, said I, replying to a cast upwards with his eyes, with which he had concluded his address – 'tis very true – and heaven be their resource who have no other but the charity of the world, the stock of which, I fear, is no way sufficient for the many *great claims* which are hourly made upon it.

As I pronounced the words *great claims*, he gave a slight glance with his eye downwards upon the sleeve of his tunic – I felt the full force of the appeal – I acknowledge it, said I – a coarse habit, and that but once in three years, with meagre diet – are no great matters; and the true point of pity is, as they can be earned in the world with so little industry, that your order should wish to procure them by pressing upon a fund which is the property of the lame, the blind, the aged, and the infirm – the captive who lies down counting over and over again the days of his afflictions, languishes also for his share of it; and had you been of the *order of mercy*, instead of the order of St Francis, poor as I am, continued I, pointing at my portmanteau, full chearfully should it have been opened to you, for the ransom of the unfortunate – The monk made me a bow – but of all others, resumed I, the unfortunate of our own country, surely, have the first rights; and I have left thousands in distress upon our own shore – The monk gave a cordial wave with his head – as much as to say, No doubt there is misery enough in every corner of the world, as well as within our convent – But we distinguish, said I, laying my hand upon the sleeve of his tunic, in return for his appeal – we distinguish, my good father! betwixt those who wish only to eat the bread of their own labour – and those who eat the bread of other people's, and have no other plan in life, but to get through it in sloth and ignorance, *for the love of God*.

The poor Franciscan made no reply: a hectic of a moment passed across his cheek, but could not tarry – Nature seemed to have done with her resentments in him; he shewed none – but letting his staff fall within his arm, he pressed both his hands with resignation upon his breast, and retired.

THE MONK

CALAIS

My heart smote me the moment he shut the door – Psha! said I with an air of carelessness, three several times – but it would not do: every ungracious syllable I had uttered, crouded back into my imagination: I reflected, I had no right over the poor Franciscan, but to deny him; and that the punishment of that was enough to the disappointed without the addition of unkind language – I considered his grey hairs – his courteous figure seemed to re-enter, and gently ask me what injury he had done me? – and why I could use him thus? – I would have given twenty livres for an advocate – I have behaved very ill; said I within myself; but I have only just set out upon my travels; and shall learn better manners as I get along.

THE DESOBLIGEANT

CALAIS

When a man is discontented with himself, it has one advantage however, that it puts him into an excellent frame of mind for making a bargain. Now there being no travelling through France and Italy without a chaise – and nature generally prompting us to the thing we are fittest for, I walked out into the coach-yard to buy or hire something of that kind to my purpose: an old Desobligeant* in the furthest corner of the court, hit my fancy at first sight, so I instantly got into it, and finding it in tolerable harmony with my feelings, I ordered the waiter to call Monsieur Dessein[4] the master of the hotel – but Monsieur Dessein being gone to vespers, and not caring to face the Franciscan, whom I saw on the opposite side of the court, in conference with a lady just arrived, at the inn – I drew

* A chaise, so called in France, from its holding but one person.

the taffeta curtain betwixt us, and being determined to write my journey, I took out my pen and ink, and wrote the preface to it in the *Desobligeant*.

PREFACE

IN THE DESOBLIGEANT

It must have been observed by many a peripatetic philosopher, That nature has set up by her own unquestionable authority certain boundaries and fences to circumscribe the discontent of man: she has effected her purpose in the quietest and easiest manner by laying him under almost insuperable obligations to work out his ease, and to sustain his sufferings at home. It is there only that she has provided him with the most suitable objects to partake of his happiness, and bear a part of that burden which, in all countries and ages, has ever been too heavy for one pair of shoulders. 'Tis true we are endued with an imperfect power of spreading our happiness sometimes beyond *her* limits, but 'tis so ordered, that, from the want of languages, connections, and dependencies, and from the difference in education, customs, and habits, we lie under so many impediments in communicating our sensations out of our own sphere, as often amount to a total impossibility.

It will always follow from hence, that the balance of sentimental commerce is always against the expatriated adventurer: he must buy what he has little occasion for at their own price – his conversation will seldom be taken in exchange for theirs without a large discount – and this, by the by, eternally driving him into the hands of more equitable brokers for such conversation as he can find, it requires no great spirit of divination to guess at his party –

This brings me to my point; and naturally leads me (if the see-saw of this *Desobligeant* will but let me get on) into the efficient as well as the final causes[5] of travelling –

Your idle people that leave their native country and

go abroad for some reason or reasons which may be derived from one of these general causes –

> Infirmity of body,
> Imbecility of mind, or
> Inevitable necessity.

The first two include all those who travel by land or by water, labouring with pride, curiosity, vanity or spleen, subdivided and combined *in infinitum*.

The third class includes the whole army of peregrine[6] martyrs; more especially those travellers who set out upon their travels with the benefit of the clergy, either as delinquents travelling under the direction of governors recommended by the magistrate – or young gentlemen transported by the cruelty of parents and guardians, and travelling under the direction of governors recommended by Oxford, Aberdeen and Glasgow.

There is a fourth class, but their number is so small that they would not deserve a distinction, was it not necessary in a work of this nature to observe the greatest precision and nicety, to avoid a confusion of character. And these men I speak of, are such as cross the seas, and sojourn in a land of strangers with a view of saving money for various reasons and upon various pretences: but as they might also save themselves and others a great deal of unnecessary trouble by saving their money at home – and as their reasons for travelling are the least complex of any other species of emigrants, I shall distinguish these gentlemen by the name of

> Simple Travellers.

Thus the whole circle of travellers may be reduced to the following *heads*.

> Idle Travellers,
> Inquisitive Travellers,
> Lying Travellers,

>Proud Travellers,
>Vain Travellers,
>Splenetic Travellers.

Then follow the Travellers of Necessity.
The delinquent and felonious Traveller,
The unfortunate and innocent Traveller,
The simple Traveller,
And last of all (if you please) The

Sentimental Traveller (meaning thereby myself) who have travelled, and of which I am now sitting down to give an account – as much out of *Necessity*, and the *besoin de Voyager*, as any one in the class.

I am well aware, at the same time, as both my travels and observations will be altogether of a different cast from any of my fore-runners; that I might have insisted upon a whole nitch entirely to myself – but I should break in upon the confines of the *Vain* Traveller, in wishing to draw attention towards me, till I have some better grounds for it, than the mere *Novelty of my Vehicle*.

It is sufficient for my reader, if he has been a traveller himself, that with study and reflection hereupon he may be able to determine his own place and rank in the catalogue – it will be one step towards knowing himself; as it is great odds, but he retains some tincture and resemblance, of what he imbibed or carried out, to the present hour.

The man who first transplanted the grape of Burgundy to the Cape of Good Hope (observe he was a Dutchman) never dreamt of drinking the same wine at the Cape, that the same grape produced upon the French mountains – he was too phlegmatic for that – but undoubtedly he expected to drink some sort of vinous liquor; but whether good, bad, or indifferent – he knew enough of this world to know, that it did not depend upon his choice, but that which is generally called *chance* was to decide his success: however, he hoped for the best; and in these hopes, by an intemperate confidence in the fortitude of his head, and the depth of his discretion, *Mynheer* might possibly overset both in his new vineyard; and by discovering his nakedness, become a laughing-stock to his people.

Even so it fares with the poor Traveller, sailing and posting through the politer kingdoms of the globe in pursuit of knowledge and improvements.

Knowledge and improvements are to be got by sailing and posting for that purpose; but whether useful knowledge and real improvements, is all a lottery – and even where the adventurer is successful, the acquired stock must be used with caution and sobriety to turn to any profit – but as the chances run prodigiously the other way both as to the acquisition and application, I am of opinion, That a man would act as wisely, if he could prevail upon himself to live contented without foreign knowledge or foreign improvements, especially if he lives in a country that has no absolute want of either – and indeed, much grief of heart has it oft and many a time cost me, when I have observed how many a foul step the inquisitive Traveller has measured to see sights and look into discoveries; all which, as Sancho Pança said to Don Quixote, they might have seen dry-shod at home. It is an age so full of light, that there is scarce a country or corner of Europe whose beams are not crossed and interchanged with others — Knowledge in most of its branches, and in most affairs, is like music in an Italian street, whereof those may partake, who pay nothing – But there is no nation under heaven – and God is my record, (before whose tribunal I must one day come and give an account of this work) – that I do not speak it vauntingly – But there is no nation under heaven abounding with more variety of learning – where the sciences may be more fitly wooed, or more surely won than here – where art is encouraged, and will soon rise high – where Nature (take her altogether) has so little to answer for – and, to close all, where there is more wit and variety of character to feed the mind with — Where then, my dear countrymen, are you going —

– We are only looking at this chaise, said they — Your most obedient servant, said I, skipping out of it, and pulling off my hat — We were wondering, said one of them, who, I found, was an *inquisitive traveller* – what could occasion its motion. — 'Twas the agitation, said I coolly, of writing a preface — I never heard, said the other, who was a *simple traveller*, of a preface wrote in a *Desobligeant*. — It would have been better, said I, in a *Vis a Vis*.[7]

— *As an Englishman does not travel to see Englishmen*, I retired to my room.

CALAIS

I PERCEIVED that something darkened the passage more than myself, as I stepped along it to my room; it was effectually Mons. Dessein, the master of the hotel, who had just returned from vespers, and, with his hat under his arm, was most complaisantly following me, to put me in mind of my wants. I had wrote myself pretty well out of conceit with the *Desobligeant;* and Mons. Dessein speaking of it, with a shrug, as if it would no way suit me, it immediately struck my fancy that it belonged to some *innocent traveller*, who, on his return home, had left it to Mons. Dessein's honour to make the most of. Four months had elapsed since it had finished its career of Europe in the corner of Mons. Dessein's coach-yard; and having sallied out from thence but a vampt-up business at the first, though it had been twice taken to pieces on Mount Sennis, it had not profited much by its adventures – but by none so little as the standing so many months unpitied in the corner of Mons. Dessein's coach-yard. Much indeed was not to be said for it – but something might – and when a few words will rescue misery out of her distress, I hate the man who can be a churl of them.

– Now was I the master of this hotel, said I, laying the point of my fore-finger on Mons. Dessein's breast, I would inevitably make a point of getting rid of this unfortunate *Desobligeant* — it stands swinging reproaches at you every time you pass by it ——

Mon Dieu! said Mons. Dessein – I have no interest – Except the interest, said I, which men of a certain turn of mind take, Mons. Dessein, in their own sensations – I'm persuaded, to a man who feels for others as well as for himself, every rainy night, disguise it as you will, must cast a damp upon your spirits – You suffer, Mons. Dessein, as much as the machine –

I have always observed when there is as much *sour* as *sweet* in a compliment, that an Englishman is eternally at a loss within himself, whether to take it, or let it alone: a Frenchman never is: Mons. Dessein made me a bow.

C'est bien vrai, said he – But in this case I should only exchange one disquietude for another, and with loss: figure to yourself, my dear Sir, that in giving you a chaise which would fall to pieces before you had got half way to Paris – figure to yourself how much I should suffer, in giving an ill impression of myself to a man of honour, and lying at the mercy, as I must do, *d'un homme d'esprit.*

The dose was made up exactly after my own prescription; so I could not help taking it – and returning Mons. Dessein his bow, without more casuistry we walked together towards his Remise,[8] to take a view of his magazine of chaises.

IN THE STREET

CALAIS

IT must needs be a hostile kind of a world, when the buyer (if it be but of a sorry post-chaise) cannot go forth with the seller thereof into the street to terminate the difference betwixt them, but he instantly falls into the same frame of mind and views his conventionist with the same sort of eye, as if he was going along with him to Hyde-park corner to fight a duel. For my own part, being but a poor sword's-man, and no way a match for Monsieur Dessein, I felt the rotation of all the movements within me, to which the situation is incident — I looked at Monsieur Dessein through and through – eyed him as he walked along in profile – then, *en face* – thought he looked like a Jew – then a Turk – disliked his wig – cursed him by my gods – wished him at the devil ——

– And is all this to be lighted up in the heart for a beggarly account of three or four louis-d'ors, which is the most I can be over-reached in? – Base passion! said I, turning myself about, as a man naturally does upon a sudden reverse of sentiment – base, ungentle passion! thy hand is against every man, and every man's hand against thee – Heaven forbid! said she, raising her hand up to her forehead, for I had turned full in front upon the lady whom I had seen in conference with the monk – she had followed us unperceived — Heaven forbid indeed! said I, offering her my own – she had a black pair of silk gloves open only at the thumb and two fore-fingers, so accepted it without reserve – and I led her up to the door of the Remise.

Monsieur Dessein had *diabled*⁹ the key above fifty times before he found out he had come with a wrong one in his hand: we were as impatient as himself to have it opened; and so attentive to the obstacle, that I continued holding her hand almost without knowing it; so that Monsieur Dessein left us together with her hand in mine, and with our faces turned towards the door of the Remise, and said he would be back in five minutes.

Now a colloquy of five minutes, in such a situation, is worth one of as many ages, with your faces turned towards the street: in the latter case, 'tis drawn from the objects and occurrences without – when your eyes are fixed upon a dead blank – you draw purely from yourselves. A silence of a single moment upon Monsieur Dessein's leaving us, had been fatal to the situation – she had infallibly turned about – so I begun the conversation instantly. ——

—— But what were the temptations, (as I write not to

apologize for the weaknesses of my heart in this tour, – but to give an account of them) – shall be described with the same simplicity, with which I felt them.

THE REMISE DOOR

CALAIS

WHEN I told the reader that I did not care to get out of the *Desobligeant*, because I saw the monk in close conference with a lady just arrived at the inn – I told him the truth; but I did not tell him the whole truth; for I was full as much restrained by the appearance and figure of the lady he was talking to. Suspicion crossed my brain, and said, he was telling her what had passed: something jarred upon it within me — I wished him at his convent.

When the heart flies out before the understanding, it saves the judgment a world of pains — I was certain she was of a better order of beings — however, I thought no more of her, but went on and wrote my preface.

The impression returned, upon my encounter with her in the street; a guarded frankness with which she gave me her hand, shewed, I thought, her good education and her good sense; and as I led her on, I felt a pleasurable ductility about her, which spread a calmness over all my spirits ——

– Good God! how a man might lead such a creature as this round the world with him ! —

I had not yet seen her face – 'twas not material; for the drawing was instantly set about, and long before we had got to the door of the Remise, *Fancy* had finished the whole head, and pleased herself as much with its fitting her goddess, as if she had dived into the TIBER for it —— but thou art a seduced, and a seducing slut; and albeit thou cheatest us seven times a day with thy pictures and images, yet with so many charms dost thou do it, and thou deckest out thy pictures in the shapes of so many angels of light, 'tis a shame to break with thee.

When we had got to the door of the Remise, she withdrew her hand from across her forehead, and let me see the original – it was a face of about six and twenty – of a clear transparent brown, simply set off without rouge or powder – it was not critically handsome, but there was that in it, which in the frame of mind I was in, attached me much more to it – it was interesting; I fancied it wore the characters of a widowed look, and in that state of its declension, which had passed the two first paroxysms of sorrow, and was quietly beginning to reconcile itself to its loss – but a thousand other distresses might have traced the same lines; I wished to know what they had been – and was ready to inquire, (had the same *bon ton* of conversation permitted, as in the days of Esdras[10]. — '*What aileth thee? and why art thou disquieted? and why is thy understanding troubled?*' — In a word, I felt benevolence for her; and resolved some way or other to throw in my mite of courtesy – if not of service.

Such were my temptations – and in this disposition to give way to them, was I left alone with the lady with her hand in mine, and with our faces both turned closer to the door of the Remise than what was absolutely necessary.

THE REMISE DOOR

CALAIS

THIS certainly, fair lady! said I, raising her hand up a little lightly as I begun, must be one of Fortune's whimsical doings: to take two utter strangers by their hands – of different sexes, and perhaps from different corners of the globe, and in one movement place them together in such a cordial situation, as Friendship herself could scarce have atchieved for them, had she projected it for a month –

– And your reflection upon it, shews how much, Monsieur, she has embarrassed you by the adventure. —

When the situation is, what we would wish, nothing is

so ill-timed as to hint at the circumstances which make it so: you thank Fortune, continued she – you had reason – the heart knew it, and was satisfied; and who but an English philosopher would have sent notices of it to the brain to reverse the judgment?

In saying this, she disengaged her hand with a look which I thought a sufficient commentary upon the text.

It is a miserable picture which I am going to give of the weakness of my heart, by owning, that it suffered a pain, which worthier occasions could not have inflicted. — I was mortified with the loss of her hand, and the manner in which I had lost it carried neither oil nor wine to the wound: I never felt the pain of a sheepish inferiority so miserably in my life.

The triumphs of a true feminine heart are short upon these discomfitures. In a very few seconds she laid her hand upon the cuff of my coat, in order to finish her reply; so some way or other, God knows how, I regained my situation.

—— She had nothing to add.

I forthwith began to model a different conversation for the lady, thinking from the spirit as well as moral of this, that I had been mistaken in her character; but upon turning her face towards me, the spirit which had animated the reply was fled – the muscles relaxed, and I beheld the same unprotected look of distress which first won me to her interest – melancholy! to see such sprightliness the prey of sorrow. —— I pitied her from my soul; and though it may seem ridiculous enough to a torpid heart, – I could have taken her into my arms and cherished her, though it was in the open street, without blushing.

The pulsations of the arteries along my fingers pressing across hers, told her what was passing within me: she looked down – a silence of some moments followed.

I fear, in this interval, I must have made some slight efforts towards a closer compression of her hand, from a subtle sensation I felt in the palm of my own – not as if she was going to withdraw hers – but, as if she thought about it – and I had infallibly lost it a second time, had not instinct more than reason directed me to the last resource in these dangers – to hold it loosely, and in a manner as if I was every moment going to release it, of myself; so she let it continue, till Monsieur Dessein returned with the key; and in the mean time I set myself to consider how I should undo the ill impressions which the poor monk's story, in case he had told it her, must have planted in her breast against me.

THE SNUFF-BOX

CALAIS

THE good old monk was within six paces of us, as the idea of him crossed my mind; and was advancing towards us a little out of the line, as if uncertain whether he should break in upon us or no. — He stopped, however, as soon as he came up to us, with a word of frankness; and having a horn snuff-box in his hand, he presented it open to me – You shall taste mine – said I, pulling out my box (which was a small tortoise one) and putting it into his hand – 'Tis most excellent, said the monk; Then do me the favour, I replied, to accept of the box and all, and when you take a pinch out of it, sometimes recollect it was the peace-offering of a man who once used you unkindly, but not from his heart.

The poor monk blushed as red as scarlet. *Mon Dieu!* said he, pressing his hands together – you never used me unkindly. – I should think, said the lady, he is not likely. I blushed in my turn; but from what movements, I leave to the few who feel to analyse – Excuse me, Madame, replied I — I treated him most unkindly; and from no provocations – 'Tis impossible, said the lady. – My God! cried the monk, with a warmth of asseveration which seemed not to belong to him – the fault was in me, and in the indiscretion of my zeal – the lady opposed it, and I joined with her in maintaining it was impossible, that a spirit so regulated as his, could give offence to any.

I knew not that contention could be rendered so sweet and pleasurable a thing to the nerves as I then felt it. – We remained silent, without any sensation of that foolish pain which takes place, when in such a circle you look for ten minutes in one another's faces without saying a word. Whilst this lasted, the monk rubbed his horn-box upon the sleeve of his tunic; and as soon as it had acquired a little air of brightness by the friction – he made a low bow, and said, 'twas too late to say whether it was the weakness or goodness of our tempers which had involved us in this contest – but be it as it would – he begged we might exchange boxes. — In saying this, he presented his to me with one hand, as he took mine from me in the other; and having kissed it – with a stream of good nature in his eyes, he put it into his bosom – and took his leave.

I guard this box, as I would the instrumental parts of my religion, to help my mind on to something better: in truth, I seldom go abroad without it; and oft and many a time have I called up by it the courteous spirit of its owner to regulate my own, in the justlings of the world; they had found full employment for his, as I learnt from his story, till about the forty-fifth year of his age, when upon some military services ill requited, and meeting at the same time with a disappointment in the tenderest of passions, he abandoned the sword and the sex together, and took sanctuary, not so much in his convent as in himself.

I feel a damp upon my spirits, as I am going to add, that in my last return through Calais, upon inquiring after Father Lorenzo, I heard he had been dead near three months, and was buried, not in his convent, but according to his desire, in a little cimetiery belonging to it, about two leagues off: I had a strong desire to see where they had laid him, – when, upon pulling out his little horn-box, as I sat by his grave, and plucking up a nettle or two at the head of it, which had no business to grow there, they all struck together so forcibly upon my affections, that I burst into a flood of tears — but I am as weak as a woman; and I beg the world not to smile, but pity me.

THE REMISE DOOR

CALAIS

I HAD never quitted the lady's hand all this time; and had held it so long, that it would have been indecent to have let it go, without first pressing it to my lips: the blood and spirits, which had suffered a revulsion from her, crouded back to her, as I did it.

Now the two travellers who had spoke to me in the coach-yard, happening at that crisis to be passing by, and observing our communications, naturally took it into their heads that we must be *man and wife* at least; so stopping as soon as they came up to the door of the Remise, the one of them, who was the inquisitive traveller, asked us, if we set out for Paris the next morning? – I could only answer for myself, I said; and the lady added, she was for Amiens. — We dined there yesterday, said the simple traveller – You go directly through the town, added the other, in your road to Paris. I was going to return a thousand thanks for the intelligence, *that Amiens was in the road to Paris;* but, upon pulling out my poor monk's little horn-box to take a pinch of snuff – I made them a quiet bow, and wishing them a good passage to Dover – they left us alone —

– Now where would be the harm, said I to myself, if I was to beg of this distressed lady to accept of half of my chaise? – and what mighty mischief could ensue?

Every dirty passion, and bad propensity in my nature, took the alarm, as I stated the proposition — It will oblige you to have a third horse, said AVARICE, which will put twenty livres out of your pocket. —— You know not who she is, said CAUTION – or what scrapes the affair may draw you into, whispered COWARDICE ——

Depend upon it, Yorick! said DISCRETION, 'twill be said you went off with a mistress, and came by assignation to Calais for that purpose —

– You can never after, cried HYPOCRISY aloud, shew your face in the world – or rise, quoth MEANNESS, in the church – or be anything in it, said PRIDE, but a lousy prebendary.

– But 'tis a civil thing, said I – and as I generally act from the first impulse, and therefore seldom listen to these cabals, which serve no purpose, that I know of, but to encompass the heart with adamant – I turned instantly about to the lady —

– But she had glided off unperceived, as the cause was pleading, and had made ten or a dozen paces down the street, by the time I had made the determination; so I set off after her with a long stride, to make her the proposal with the best address I was master of; but observing she walked with her cheek half resting upon the palm of her hand — with the slow, short-measured step of thoughtfulness, and with her eyes, as she went step by step, fixed upon the ground, it struck me, she was trying the same cause herself. — God help her! said I, she has some mother-in-law, or tartufish[11] aunt, or nonsensical old woman, to consult upon the occasion, as well as myself: so not caring to interrupt the processe, and deeming it more gallant to take her at discretion than by surprise, I faced about, and took a short turn or two before the door of the Remise, whilst she walked musing on one side.

IN THE STREET

CALAIS

HAVING, on first sight of the lady, settled the affair in my fancy, 'that she was of the better order of beings' – and then laid it down as a second axiom, as indisputable as the first, That she was a widow, and wore a character of distress

– I went no further; I got ground enough for the situation which pleased me – and had she remained close beside my elbow till midnight, I should have held true to my system, and considered her only under that general idea.

She had scarce got twenty paces distant from me, ere something within me called out for a more particular inquiry – it brought on the idea of a further separation – I might possibly never see her more – the heart is for saving what it can; and I wanted the traces through which my wishes might find their way to her, in case I should never rejoin her myself: in a word, I wished to know her name – her family's – her condition; and as I knew the place to which she was going, I wanted to know from whence she came: but there was no coming at all this intelligence: a hundred little delicacies stood in the way. I formed a score of different plans – There was no such thing as a man's asking her directly – the thing was impossible.

A little French *debonaire* captain, who came dancing down the street, shewed me, it was the easiest thing in the world; for popping in betwixt us, just as the lady was returning back to the door of the Remise, he introduced himself to my acquaintance, and before he had well got announced, begged I would do him the honour to present him to the lady — I had not been presented myself — so turning about to her, he did it just as well by asking her, if she had come from Paris? —— No: she was going that rout, she said. — *Vous n'etez pas de Londre?* —— She was not, she replied. – Then Madame must have come through Flanders. *Apparemment vous etez Flammande?* said the French captain. – The lady answered she was. – *Peut-être, de Lisle?* added he – She said, she was not of Lisle. – Nor Arras? — nor Cambray? — nor Ghent? – nor Brussels? She answered, she was of Brussels.

He had had the honour, he said, to be at the bombardment of it last war – that it was finely situated, *pour cela* – and full of noblesse when the Imperialists were driven out by the French (the lady made a slight curtsy) – so giving her an account of the affair, and of the share he had had in it – he begged the honour to know her name – so made his bow.

—— *Et Madame a son Mari?* — said he, looking back when he had made two steps – and without staying for an answer – danced down the street.

Had I served seven years apprenticeship to good breeding, I could not have done as much.

THE REMISE

CALAIS

As the little French captain left us, Mons. Dessein came up with the key of the Remise in his hand, and forthwith let us into his magazine of chaises.

The first object which caught my eye, as Mons. Dessein opened the door of the Remise, was another old tattered *Desobligeant*: and notwithstanding it was the exact picture of that which had hit my fancy so much in the coach-yard but an hour before – the very sight of it stirred up a disagreeable sensation within me now; and I thought 'twas a churlish beast into whose heart the idea could first enter, to construct such a machine; nor had I much more charity for the man who could think of using it.

I observed the lady was as little taken with it as myself: so Mons. Dessein led us on to a couple of chaises which stood abreast, telling us, as he recommended them, that they had been purchased by my Lord A. and B. to go the *grand tour*, but had gone no further than Paris, so were in all respects as good as new – They were too good – so I passed on to a third, which stood behind, and forthwith began to chaffer for the price – But 'twill scarce hold two, said I, opening the door and getting in – Have the goodness, Madam, said Mons. Dessein, offering his arm, to step in – The lady hesitated half a second, and stepped in; and

the waiter that moment beckoning to speak to Mons.
Dessein, he shut the door of the chaise upon us, and left
us.

THE REMISE

CALAIS

C'est bien comique, 'tis very droll, said the lady smiling,
from the reflection that this was the second time we had
been left together by a parcel of nonsensical contingencies
– *c'est bien comique*, said she –

– There wants nothing, said I, to make it so, but the
comic use which the gallantry of a Frenchman would put
it to – to make love the first moment, and an offer of his
person the second.

'Tis their *fort:* replied the lady.

It is supposed so at least – and how it has come to pass,
continued I, I know not; but they have certainly got the
credit of understanding more of love, and making it better
than any other nation upon earth: but for my own part I
think them errant bunglers, and in truth the worst set of
marksmen that ever tried Cupid's patience.

– To think of making love by *sentiments!*

I should as soon think of making a genteel suit of cloaths
out of remnants: – and to do it – pop – at first sight by
declaration – is submitting the offer and themselves with
it, to be sifted, with all their *pours* and *contres*, by an un-
heated mind.

The lady attended as if she expected I should go on.

Consider then, Madam, continued I, laying my hand
upon hers –

That grave people hate Love for the name's sake –

That selfish people hate it for their own –

Hypocrites for heaven's –

And that all of us, both old and young, being ten times
worse frightened than hurt by the very *report* – What a

want of knowledge in this branch of commerce a man betrays, whoever lets the word come out of his lips, till an hour or two at least after the time, that his silence upon it becomes tormenting. A course of small, quiet attentions, not so pointed as to alarm – nor so vague as to be misunderstood, – with now and then a look of kindness, and little or nothing said upon it – leaves Nature for your mistress, and she fashions it to her mind. –

Then I solemnly declare, said the lady, blushing – you have been making love to me all this while.

THE REMISE

CALAIS

MONSIEUR DESSEIN came back to let us out of the chaise, and acquaint the lady, the Count de L— her brother was just arrived at the hotel. Though I had infinite good-will for the lady, I cannot say, that I rejoiced in my heart at the event – and could not help telling her so – for it is fatal to a proposal, Madam, said I, that I was going to make to you –

– You need not tell me what the proposal was, said she, laying her hand upon both mine, as she interrupted me. – A man, my good Sir, has seldom an offer of kindness to make to a woman, but she has a presentiment of it some moments before –

Nature arms her with it, said I, for immediate preservation – But I think, said she, looking in my face, I had no evil to apprehend – and to deal frankly with you, had determined to accept it. — If I had – (she stopped a moment) – I believe your good-will would have drawn a story from me, which would have made pity the only dangerous thing in the journey.

In saying this, she suffered me to kiss her hand twice, and with a look of sensibility mixed with a concern she got out of the chaise – and bid adieu.

IN THE STREET
CALAIS

I never finished a twelve-guinea bargain so expeditiously in my life: my time seemed heavy upon the loss of the lady, and knowing every moment of it would be as two, till I put myself into motion – I ordered post-horses directly, and walked towards the hotel.

Lord! said I, hearing the town clock strike four, and recollecting that I had been little more than a single hour in Calais –

– What a large volume of adventures may be grasped within this little span of life by him who interests his heart in everything, and who having eyes to see, what time and chance are perpetually holding out to him as he journeyeth on his way, misses nothing he can *fairly* lay his hands on. —

– If this won't turn out something – another will – no matter – 'tis an assay upon human nature – I get my labour for my pains – 'tis enough – the pleasure of the experiment has kept my senses, and the best part of my blood awake, and laid the gross to sleep.

I pity the man who can travel from *Dan* to *Beersheba*,[12] and cry, 'Tis all barren — and so it is; and so is all the world to him who will not cultivate the fruits it offers. I declare, said I, clapping my hands chearily together, that was I in a desert, I would find out wherewith in it to call forth my affections — If I could not do better, I would fasten them upon some sweet myrtle, or seek some melancholy cypress to connect myself to — I would court their shade, and greet them kindly for their protection – I would cut my name upon them, and swear they were the loveliest trees throughout the desert: if their leaves withered, I would teach myself to mourn, and when they rejoiced, I would rejoice along with them.

The learned Smelfungus[13] travelled from Boulogne to Paris – from Paris to Rome – and so on – but he set out with the spleen and jaundice, and every object he passed by was discoloured or distorted — He wrote an account of them, but 'twas nothing but the account of his miserable feelings.

I met Smelfungus in the grand portico of the Pantheon – he was just coming out of it – *'Tis nothing but a huge cock pit,* said he — I wish you had said nothing worse of the Venus of Medicis, replied I – for in passing through Florence, I had heard he had fallen foul upon the goddess, and used her worse than a common strumpet, without the least provocation in nature.

I popped upon Smelfungus again at Turin, in his return home; and a sad tale of sorrowful adventures had he to tell, 'wherein he spoke of moving accidents by flood and field, and of the cannibals which each other eat: the Anthropophagi'[14] — he had been flea'd alive, and bedeviled, and used worse than St Bartholomew,[15] at every stage he had come at –

– I'll tell it, cried Smelfungus, to the world. You had better tell it, said I, to your physician.

Mundungus,[16] with an immense fortune, made the whole tour; going on from Rome to Naples – from Naples to Venice – from Venice to Vienna – to Dresden, to Berlin, without one generous connection or pleasurable anecdote to tell of; but he had travelled straight on, looking neither to his right hand or his left, lest Love or Pity should seduce him out of his road.

Peace be to them! if it is to be found; but heaven itself, was it possible to get there with such tempers, would want objects to give it – every gentle spirit would come flying upon the wings of Love to hail their arrival — Nothing would the souls of Smelfungus and Mundungus hear of, but fresh anthems of joy, fresh raptures of love, and fresh congratulations of their common felicity — I heartily pity them: they have brought up no faculties for this work; and was the happiest mansion in heaven to be allotted to

* *Vide* S — 's Travels.

Smelfungus and Mundungus, they would be so far from being happy, that the souls of Smelfungus and Mundungus would do penance there to all eternity.

MONTRIUL

I HAD once lost my portmanteau from behind my chaise, and twice got out in the rain, and one of the times up to the knees in dirt, to help the postillion to tie it on, without being able to find out what was wanting — Nor was it till I got to Montriul, upon the landlord's asking me if I wanted not a servant, that it occurred to me, that that was the very thing.

A servant! That I do most sadly, quoth I — Because, Monsieur, said the landlord, there is a clever young fellow, who would be very proud of the honour to serve an Englishman — But why an English one, more than any other? — They are so generous, said the landlord – I'll be shot if this is not a livre out of my pocket, quoth I to myself, this very night — But they have wherewithal to be so, Monsieur, added he – Set down one livre more for that, quoth I — It was but last night, said the landlord, *qu'un my Lord Anglois presentoit un ecu a la fille de chambre – Tant pis, pour Madamoiselle Janatone*, said I.

Now Janatone being the landlord's daughter, and the landlord supposing I was young in French, took the liberty to inform me, I should not have said *tant pis* – but, *tant mieux. Tant mieux, toujours, Monsieur*, said he, when there is any thing to be got – *tant pis*, when there is nothing. It comes to the same thing, said I. *Pardonnez moi*, said the landlord.

I cannot take a fitter opportunity to observe once for all, that *tant pis* and *tant mieux* being two of the great hinges in French conversation, a stranger would do well to set himself right in the use of them, before he gets to Paris.

A prompt French Marquis at our ambassador's table

demanded of Mr H—, if he was H—[17] the poet? No, said H— mildly – *Tant pis*, replied the Marquis.

It is H— the historian, said another – *Tant mieux*, said the Marquis. And Mr H—, who is a man of an excellent heart, returned thanks for both.

When the landlord had set me right in this matter, he called in La Fleur, which was the name of the young man he had spoke of – saying only first, That as for his talents, he would presume to say nothing – Monsieur was the best judge what would suit him; but for the fidelity of La Fleur, he would stand responsible in all he was worth.

The landlord delivered this in a manner which instantly set my mind to the business I was upon – and La Fleur, who stood waiting without, in that breathless expectation which every son of nature of us have felt in our turns, came in.

MONTRIUL

I AM apt to be taken with all kinds of people at first sight; but never more so, than when a poor devil comes to offer his service to so poor a devil as myself; and as I know this weakness, I always suffer my judgment to draw back something on that very account – and this more or less, according to the mood I am in, and the case – and I may add the gender too, of the person I am to govern.

When La Fleur entered the room, after every discount I could make for my soul, the genuine look and air of the fellow determined the matter at once in his favour; so I hired him first – and then began to inquire what he could do: But I shall find out his talents, quoth I, as I want them – besides, a Frenchman can do everything.

Now poor La Fleur could do nothing in the world but beat a drum, and play a march or two upon the fife. I was determined to make his talents do; and can't say my weakness was ever so insulted by my wisdom, as in the attempt.

La Fleur had set out early in life, as gallantly as most

Frenchmen do, with *serving* for a few years; at the end of which, having satisfied the sentiment, and found, moreover, That the honour of beating a drum was likely to be its own reward, as it opened no further track of glory to him – he retired *à ses terres*, and lived *comme il plaisoit à Dieu* — that is to say, upon nothing.

– And so, quoth *Wisdome*, you have hired a drummer to attend you in this tour of yours through France and Italy! Psha! said I, and do not one half of our gentry go with a humdrum *compagnon du voyage* the same round, and have the piper and the devil and all to pay besides? When a man can extricate himself with an *equivoque* in such an unequal match – he is not ill off — But you can do something else, La Fleur? said I — *O qu'oui!* – he could make spatterdashes,[18] and play a little upon the fiddle — Bravo! said Wisdome — Why, I play a bass myself, said I – we shall do very well. You can shave, and dress a wig a little, La Fleur? — He had all the dispositions in the world – It is enough for heaven! said I, interrupting him – and ought to be enough for me — So supper coming in, and having a frisky English spaniel on one side of my chair, and a French valet, with as much hilarity in his countenance as ever nature painted in one, on the other – I was satisfied to my heart's content with my empire; and if monarchs knew what they would be at, they might be as satisfied as I was.

MONTRIUL

As La Fleur[19] went the whole tour of France and Italy with me, and will be often upon the stage, I must interest the reader a little further in his behalf, by saying, that I had never less reason to repent of the impulses which generally do determine me, than in regard to this fellow – he was a faithful, affectionate, simple soul as ever trudged after the heels of a philosopher; and notwithstanding his talents of drum-beating and spatterdash-making, which, though very good in themselves, happened to be of no great service to me, yet was I hourly recompenced by the festivity of his temper – it supplied all defects – I had a constant resource in his looks in all difficulties and distresses of my own – I was going to have added, of his too; but La Fleur was out of the reach of everything; for whether 'twas hunger or thirst, or cold or nakedness, or watchings, or whatever stripes of ill luck La Fleur met with in our journeyings, there was no index in his physiognomy to point them out by – he was eternally the same; so that if I am a piece of a philosopher, which Satan now and then puts it into my head I am – it always mortifies the pride of the conceit, by reflecting how much I owe to the complexional philosophy of this poor fellow, for shaming me into one of a better kind. With all this, La Fleur had a small cast of the coxcomb – but he seemed at first sight to be more a coxcomb of nature than of art; and before I had been three days in Paris with him – he seemed to be no coxcomb at all.

MONTRIUL

THE next morning La Fleur entering upon his employment, I delivered to him the key of my portmanteau with an inventory of my half a dozen shirts and silk pair of breeches; and bid him fasten all upon the chaise – get the horses put to – and desire the landlord to come in with his bill.

C'est un garçon de bonne fortune, said the landlord, pointing through the window to half a dozen wenches who had got round about La Fleur, and were most kindly taking their leave of him, as the postillion was leading out the horses. La Fleur kissed all their hands round and round again, and thrice he wiped his eyes, and thrice he promised he would bring them all pardons from Rome.

The young fellow, said the landlord, is beloved by all

the town, and there is scarce a corner in Montriul where the want of him will not be felt: he has but one misfortune in the world, continued he, 'He is always in love.' — I am heartily glad of it, said I, — 'twill save me the trouble every night of putting my breeches under my head. In saying this, I was making not so much La Fleur's eloge, as my own, having been in love with one princess or another almost all my life, and I hope I shall go on so, till I die, being firmly persuaded, that if ever I do a mean action, it must be in some interval betwixt one passion and another: whilst this interregnum lasts, I always perceive my heart locked up — I can scarce find in it, to give Misery a sixpence; and therefore I always get out of it as fast as I can, and the moment I am rekindled, I am all generosity and good will again; and would do anything in the world either for, or with anyone, if they will but satisfy me there is no sin in it.

– But in saying this – surely I am commending the passion – not myself.

A FRAGMENT

——THE town of Abdera,[20] notwithstanding Democritus lived there trying all the powers of irony and laughter to reclaim it, was the vilest and most profligate town in all Thrace. What for poisons, conspiracies, and assassinations – libels, pasquinades[21] and tumults, there was no going there by day – 'twas worse by night.

Now, when things were at the worst, it came to pass, that the *Andromeda* of Euripides being represented at Abdera, the whole orchestra was delighted with it: but of all the passages which delighted them, nothing operated more upon their imaginations, than the tender strokes of nature which the poet had wrought up in that pathetic speech of Perseus,

O Cupid! prince of God and men, &c.

Every man almost spoke pure iambics the next day and talked of nothing but Perseus his pathetic address – 'O Cupid! prince of God and men' — in every street of Abdera, in every house – 'O Cupid! Cupid!' – in every mouth, like the natural notes of some sweet melody which drops from it whether it will nor no – nothing but 'Cupid! Cupid! prince of God and men' — The fire caught – and the whole city, like the heart of one man, opened itself to Love.

No pharmacopolist could sell one grain of helebore[22] – not a single armourer had a heart to forge one instrument of death – Friendship and Virtue met together, and kissed each other in the street – the golden age returned, and hung o'er the town of Abdera – every Abderite took his oaten pipe, and every Abderitish woman left her purple web, and chastely sat her down and listened to the song —

'Twas only in the power, says the Fragment, of the God whose empire extendeth from heaven to earth, and even to the depths of the sea, to have done this.

MONTRIUL

WHEN all is ready, and every article is disputed and paid for in the inn, unless you are a little soured by the adventure, there is always a matter to compound at the door, before you can get into your chaise; and that is with the sons and daughters of poverty, who surround you. Let no man say, 'let them go to the devil' – 'tis a cruel journey to send a few miserables, and they have had sufferings enow without it: I always think it better to take a few sous out in my hand; and I would counsel every gentle traveller to do so likewise; he need not be so exact in setting down his motives for giving them – they will be registered elsewhere.

For my own part, there is no man gives so little as I do;

for few that I know have so little to give: but as this was the first public act of my charity in France, I took the more notice of it.

A well-a-way! said I. I have but eight sous in the world, shewing them in my hand, and there are eight poor men and eight poor women for 'em.

A poor tattered soul without a shirt on instantly withdrew his claim, by retiring two steps out of the circle, and making a disqualifying bow on his part. Had the whole parterre cried out, *Place aux dames*, with one voice, it would not have conveyed the sentiment of a deference for the sex with half the effect.

Just heaven! for what wise reasons hast thou ordered it, that beggary and urbanity, which are at such variance in other countries, should find a way to be at unity in this?

– I insisted upon presenting him with a single sous, merely for his *politesse*.

A poor little dwarfish brisk fellow, who stood over-against me in the circle, putting something first under his arm, which had once been a hat, took his snuff-box out of his pocket, and generously offered a pinch on both sides of him: it was a gift of consequence, and modestly declined — The poor little fellow pressed it upon them with a nod of welcomeness — *Prenez en – prenez*, said he, looking another way; so they each took a pinch — Pity thy box should ever want one! said I to myself; so I put a couple of sous into it – taking a small pinch out of his box, to enhance their value, as I did it — He felt the weight of the second obligation more than that of the first – 'twas doing him an honour – the other was only doing him a charity – and he made me a bow to the ground for it.

– Here! said I to an old soldier with one hand, who had been campaigned and worn out to death in the service – here's a couple of sous for thee. *Vive le Roi!* said the old soldier.

I had then but three sous left: so I gave one, simply *pour l'amour de Dieu*, which was the footing on which it was begged – The poor woman had a dislocated hip; so it could not be well, upon any other motive.

Mon cher et très charitable Monsieur — There's no opposing this, said I.

My Lord Anglois – the very sound was worth the money – so I gave *my last sous for it*. But in the eagerness of giving, I had overlooked a *pauvre honteux*, who had no one to ask a sous for him, and who, I believed, would have perished, ere he could have asked one for himself: he stood by the chaise a little without the circle, and wiped a tear from a face which I thought had seen better days — Good God! said I – and I have not one single sous left to give him – But you have a thousand! cried all the powers of nature, stirring within me – so I gave him – no matter what – I am ashamed to say *how much*, now – and was ashamed to think, how little, then: so if the reader can form any conjecture of my disposition, as these two fixed points are given him, he may judge within a livre or two what was the precise sum.

I could afford nothing for the rest, but, *Dieu vous benisse* — *Et le bon Dieu vous benisse encore* – said the old soldier, the dwarf, &c. The *pauvre honteux* could say nothing – he pulled out a little handkerchief, and wiped his face as he turned away – and I thought he thanked me more than them all.

THE BIDET

HAVING settled all these little matters, I got into my post-chaise with more ease than ever I got into a post-chaise in my life; and La Fleur having got one large jack-boot on the far side of a little *bidet*,* and another on this (for I count nothing of his legs) – he cantered away before me as happy and as perpendicular as a prince. —

— But what is happiness! what is grandeur in this painted

* Post-horse.

scene of life! A dead ass, before we had got a league, put a sudden stop to La Fleur's career – his bidet would not pass by it – a contention arose betwixt them, and the poor fellow was kicked out of his jack-boots the very first kick.

La Fleur bore his fall like a French christian, saying neither more or less upon it, than, *Diable!* so presently got up and came to the charge again astride his bidet, beating him up to it as he would have beat his drum.

The bidet flew from one side of the road to the other, then back again – then this way – then that way, and in short every way but by the dead ass. — La Fleur insisted upon the thing – and the bidet threw him.

What's the matter, La Fleur, said I, with this bidet of thine? — *Monsieur*, said he, *c'est un cheval le plus opiniâtré du monde* — Nay, if he is a conceited beast, he must go his own way, replied I – so La Fleur got off him, and giving him a good sound lash, the bidet took me at my word, and away he scampered back to Montriul. — *Peste!* said La Fleur.

It is not *mal à propos* to take notice here, that though La Fleur availed himself but of two different terms of exclamation in this encounter – namely, *Diable!* and *Peste!* that there are nevertheless three, in the French language; like the positive, comparative, and superlative, one or the other of which serve for every unexpected throw of the dice in life.

Le Diable! which is the first and positive degree, is generally used upon ordinary emotions of the mind, where small things only fall out contrary to your expectations – such as – the throwing once doublets[23] – La Fleur's being kicked off his horse, and so forth – cuckoldom, for the same reason, is always – *Le Diable!*

But in cases where the cast has something provoking in it, as in that of the bidet's running away after, and leaving La Fleur aground in jack-boots – 'tis the second degree.

'Tis then *Peste!*

And for the third —

— But here my heart is wrung with pity and fellow-feeling, when I reflect what miseries must have been their lot, and how bitterly so refined a people must have smarted, to have forced them upon the use of it. ——

Grant me, O ye powers which touch the tongue with eloquence in distress! — whatever is my *cast*,[24] Grant me but decent words to exclaim in, and I will give my nature way.

– But as these were not to be had in France, I resolved to take every evil just as it befel me without any exclamation at all.

La Fleur, who had made no such covenant with himself, followed the bidet with his eyes till it was got out of sight – and then, you may imagine, if you please, with what word he closed the whole affair.

As there was no hunting down a frightened horse in jack-boots, there remained no alternative but taking La Fleur either behind the chaise, or into it. —

I preferred the latter, and in half an hour we got to the post-house at Nampont.

NAMPONT

THE DEAD ASS

– And this, said he, putting the remains of a crust into this wallet – and this, should have been thy portion, said he, hadst thou been alive to have shared it with me. I thought by the accent, it had been an apostrophe to his child; but 'twas to his ass, and to the very ass we had seen dead in the road, which had occasioned La Fleur's misadventure. The man seemed to lament it much; and it instantly brought into my mind Sancho's lamentation for his; but he did it with more true touches of nature.

The mourner was sitting upon a stone bench at the door, with the ass's pannel and its bridle on one side, which he took up from time to time – then laid them down – looked at them, and shook his head. He then took his crust of bread out of his wallet again, as if to eat it; held it some time in his hand – then laid it upon the bit of his ass's bridle – looked wistfully at the little arrangement he had made – and then gave a sigh.

The simplicity of his grief drew numbers about him, and La Fleur amongst the rest, whilst the horses were getting ready; as I continued sitting in the post-chaise, I could see and hear over their heads.

– He said he had come last from Spain, where he had been from the furthest borders of Franconia; and had got so far on his return home, when his ass died. Every one seemed desirous to know what business could have taken so old and poor a man so far a journey from his own home.

It had pleased heaven, he said, to bless him with three sons, the finest lads in all Germany; but having in one week lost two of the eldest of them by the small-pox, and the youngest falling ill of the same distemper, he was afraid of being bereft of them all; and made a vow, if Heaven would not take him from him also, he would go in gratitude to St Iago in Spain.

When the mourner got thus far on his story, he stopped to pay nature her tribute – and wept bitterly.

He said, Heaven had accepted the conditions, and that he had set out from his cottage with this poor creature, who had been a patient partner of his journey – that it had eat the same bread with him all the way, and was unto him as a friend.

Everybody who stood about, heard the poor fellow with concern — La Fleur offered him money. — The mourner said he did not want it – it was not the value of the ass – but the loss of him. — The ass, he said, he was assured loved him – and upon this told them a long story of a mischance upon their passage over the Pyrenean mountains which had separated them from each other three days; during which time the ass had sought for him as much as he

63

had sought the ass, and that they had neither scarce eat or drank till they met.

Thou hast one comfort, friend, said I, at least, in the loss of thy poor beast; I'm sure thou hast been a merciful master to him. — Alas! said the mourner, I thought so, when he was alive – but now that he is dead, I think otherwise. — I fear the weight of myself and my afflictions together have been too much for him – they have shortened the poor creature's days, and I fear I have them to answer for. – Shame on the world! said I to myself – Did we love each other, as this poor soul but loved his ass – 'twould be something. —

NAMPONT

THE POSTILLION

THE concern which the poor fellow's story threw me into, required some attention; the postillion paid not the least to it, but set off upon the *pavé* in a full gallop.

The thirstiest soul in the most sandy desert of Arabia could not have wished more for a cup of cold water, than mine did for grave and quiet movements; and I should have had an high opinion of the postillion had he but stolen off with me in something like a pensive pace. — On the contrary, as the mourner finished his lamentation, the fellow gave an unfeeling lash to each of his beasts, and set off clattering like a thousand devils.

I called to him as loud as I could, for heaven's sake to go slower – and the louder I called, the more unmercifully he galloped. — The deuce take him and his galloping too – said I – he'll go on tearing my nerves to pieces till he has worked me into a foolish passion, and then he'll go slow, that I may enjoy the sweets of it.

The postillion managed the point to a miracle: by the time he had got to the foot of a steep hill about half a league from Nampont, – he had put me out of temper with him – and then with myself, for being so!

My case then required a different treatment; and a good rattling gallop would have been of real service to me. —

– Then, prithee get on – get on, my good lad, said I.

The postillion pointed to the hill – I then tried to return back to the story of the poor German and his ass – but I had broke the clue – and could no more get into it again, than the postillion could into a trot. —

— The deuce go, said I, with it all! Here am I sitting as candidly disposed to make the best of the worst, as ever wight was, and all runs counter.

There is one sweet lenitive at least for evils, which nature holds out to us; so I took it kindly at her hands, and fell asleep; and the first word which roused me was *Amiens.*

— Bless me! said I, rubbing my eyes – this is the very town where my poor lady is to come.

AMIENS

THE words were scarce out of my mouth, when the Count de L***'s post-chaise, with his sister in it, drove hastily by: she had just time to make me a bow of recognition – and of that particular kind of it, which told me she had not yet done with me. She was as good as her look; for, before I had quite finished my supper, her brother's servant came into the room with a billet, in which she said, she had taken the liberty to charge me with a letter, which I was to present myself to Madame R*** the first morning I had nothing to do at Paris. There was only added, she was sorry, but from what *penchant* she had not considered, that she had been prevented telling me her story – that she still owed it me; and if my rout should ever lay through Brussels, and I had not by then forgot the name of Madame de L*** – that Madame de L*** would be glad to discharge her obligation.

Then I will meet thee, said I, fair spirit! at Brussels –
'tis only returning from Italy through Germany to Holland, by the rout of Flanders, home – 'twill scarce be ten
posts out of my way; but were it ten thousand! with
what a moral delight will it crown my journey, in sharing
in the sickening incidents of a tale of misery told to me by
such a sufferer? to see her weep! and though I cannot dry
up the fountain of her tears, what an exquisite sensation
is there still left, in wiping them away from off the cheeks
of the first and fairest of women, as I'm sitting with my
handkerchief in my hand in silence the whole night besides her.

There was nothing wrong in the sentiment; and yet I
instantly reproached my heart with it in the bitterest and
most reprobate of expressions.

It had ever, as I told the reader, been one of the singular blessings of my life, to be almost every hour of it
miserably in love with some one; and my last flame happening to be blown out by a whiff of jealousy on the sudden
turn of a corner, I had lighted it up afresh at the pure
taper of Eliza but about three months before – swearing
as I did it, that it should last me through the whole journey — Why should I dissemble the matter? I had sworn to
her eternal fidelity – she had a right to my whole heart
– to divide my affections was to lessen them – to expose
them, was to risk them: where there is risk, there may be
loss: – and what wilt thou have, Yorick! to answer to a
heart so full of trust and confidence – so good, so gentle
and unreproaching?

—I will not go to Brussels, replied I, interrupting myself – but my imagination went on – I recalled her looks
at that crisis of our separation when neither of us had
power to say Adieu! I looked at the picture she had tied
in a black ribband about my neck – and blushed as I
looked at it – I would have given the world to have kissed
it, – but was ashamed — And shall this tender flower, said

I, pressing it between my hands – shall it be smitten to its very root – and smitten, Yorick! by thee, who hast promised to shelter it in thy breast?

Eternal fountain of happiness! said I, kneeling down upon the ground – be thou my witness – and every pure spirit which tastes it, be my witness also, That I would not travel to Brussels, unless Eliza went along with me, did the road lead me towards heaven.

In transports of this kind, the heart, in spite of the understanding, will always say too much.

THE LETTER

AMIENS

FORTUNE had not smiled upon La Fleur; for he had been unsuccessful in his feats of chivalry — and not one thing had offered to signalize his zeal of my service from the time he had entered into it, which was almost four and twenty hours. The poor soul burned with impatience; and the Count de L***'s servant's coming with the letter, being the first practicable occasion which offered, La Fleur had laid hold of it, and in order to do honour to his master, had taken him into a back parlour in the Auberge, and treated him with a cup or two of the best wine in Picardy; and the Count de L***'s servant in return, and not to be behind-hand in politeness with La Fleur, had taken him back with him to the Count's hôtel. La Fleur's *prevenancy*[25] (for there was a passport in his very looks) soon set every servant in the kitchen at ease with him; and as a Frenchman, whatever be his talents, has no sort of prudery in shewing them, La Fleur, in less than five minutes, had pulled out his fife, and leading off the dance himself with the first note, set the *fille de chambre*, the *maitre d'hôtel*, the cook, the scullion, and all the houshold, dogs and cats, besides an old monkey, a dancing: I suppose there never was a merrier kitchen since the flood.

Madame de L***, in passing from her brother's apartments to her own, hearing so much jollity below stairs, rung up her *fille de chambre* to ask about it; and hearing it was the English gentleman's servant who had set the whole house merry with his pipe, she ordered him up.

As the poor fellow could not present himself empty, he had loadened himself in going upstairs with a thousand compliments to Madame de L***, on the part of his master – added a long apocrypha of inquiries about Madame de L***'s health – told her, that Monsieur his master was *au desespoire* for her re-establishment from the fatigues of her journey – and, to close all, that Monsieur had received the letter which Madame had done him the honour – And he has done me the honour, said Madame de L***, interrupting La Fleur, to send a billet in return.

Madame de L*** had said this with such a tone of reliance upon the fact, that La Fleur had not power to disappoint her expectations – he trembled for my honour – and possibly might not altogether be unconcerned for his own, as a man capable of being attached to a master who could be wanting *en egards vis-à-vis d'une femme;* so that when Madame de L*** asked La Fleur if he had brought a letter, *O qu'oui,* said La Fleur: so laying down his hat upon the ground, and taking hold of the flap of his right side pocket with his left hand, he began to search for the letter with his right – then contrary-wise – *Diable!* – then sought every pocket – pocket by pocket, round, not forgetting his fob — *Peste!* – then La Fleur emptied them upon the floor – pulled out a dirty cravat – a handkerchief – a comb – a whip-lash – a night-cap – then gave a peep into his hat — *Quelle etourderie!*[26] He had left the letter upon the table in the Auberge – he would run for it, and be back with it in three minutes.

I had just finished my supper when La Fleur came in to give me an account of his adventure: he told the whole story simply as it was; and only added, that if Monsieur had forgot (*par hazard*) to answer Madame's letter, the arrangement gave him an opportunity to recover the *faux pas* – and if not, that things were only as they were.

Now I was not altogether sure of my *etiquette*, whether I ought to have wrote or no; but if I had — a devil himself could not have been angry: 'twas but the officious zeal of a well-meaning creature for my honour; and however he might have mistook the road – or embarrassed me in so doing – his heart was in no fault — I was under no necessity to write – and what weighed more than all – he did not look as if he had done amiss.

— 'Tis all very well, La Fleur, said I – 'Twas sufficient. La Fleur flew out of the room like lightening, and returned with pen, ink, and paper, in his hand; and coming up to the table, laid them close before me, with such a delight in his countenance, that I could not help taking up the pen.

I begun and begun again; and though I had nothing to say, and that nothing might have been expressed in half a dozen lines, I made half a dozen different beginnings, and could no way please myself.

In short, I was in no mood to write.

La Fleur stepped out and brought a little water in a glass to dilute my ink – then fetched sand and seal-wax — It was all one: I wrote, and blotted, and tore off, and burnt, and wrote again – *Le Diable l'emporte!* said I half to myself – I cannot write this self-same letter; throwing the pen down despairingly as I said it.

As soon as I had cast down the pen, La Fleur advanced with the most respectful carriage up to the table, and making a thousand apologies for the liberty he was going to take, told me he had a letter in his pocket wrote by a drummer in his regiment to a corporal's wife, which, he durst say, would suit the occasion.

I had a mind to let the poor fellow have his humour — Then prithee, said I, let me see it.

La Fleur instantly pulled out a little dirty pocket-book crammed full of small letters and billet-doux in a sad condition, and laying it upon the table, and then untying the string which held them all together, run them over one by one, till he came to the letter in question—*La voila!* said he, clapping his hands: so unfolding it first, he laid it before me, and retired three steps from the table whilst I read it.

THE LETTER

MADAME,

JE suis penetré de la douleur la plus vive, et reduit en même temps au desespoir ce retour imprevû du Corporal qui rend notre entrevue de ce soir la chose du monde la plus impossible.

Mais vive la joie! et toute la mienne sera de penser à vous.

L'amour n'est *rien* sans sentiment.

Et le sentiment est encore *moins* sans amour.

On dit qu'on ne doit jamais se desesperer.

On dit aussi que Monsieur le Corporal monte la garde Mercredi: alors ce sera mon tour.

Chacun a son tour.

En attendant – Vive l'amour! et vive la bagatelle!

Je suis, MADAME,

Avec toutes les sentiments les plus respecteux et les plus tendres tout à vous,

JACQUES ROQUE

It was but changing the Corporal into the Count – and saying nothing about mounting guard on Wednesday – and the letter was neither right or wrong – so to gratify the poor fellow, who stood trembling for my honour, his own, and the honour of his letter, – I took the cream gently off it, and whipping it up in my own way – I sealed it up and sent him with it to Madame de L*** – and the next morning we pursued our journey to Paris.

PARIS

WHEN a man can contest the point by dint of equipage, and carry on all floundering before him with half a dozen lackies and a couple of cooks – 'tis very well in such a place as Paris – he may drive in at which end of a street he will.

A poor prince who is weak in cavalry, and whose whole infantry does not exceed a single man, had best quit the field; and signalize himself in the cabinet,[27] if he can get up into it – I say *up into it* – for there is no descending perpendicular amongst 'em with a *'Me voici! mes enfants'* – here I am – whatever many may think.

I own my first sensations, as soon as I was left solitary and alone in my own chamber in the hotel, were far from being so flattering as I had prefigured them. I walked up gravely to the window in my dusty black coat, and looking through the glass saw all the world in yellow, blue, and green, running at the ring of pleasure. — The old with broken lances, and in helmets which had lost their vizards – the young in armour bright which shone like gold, beplumed with each gay feather of the east — all — all tilting at it like fascinated knights in tournaments of yore for fame and love. —

Alas, poor Yorick! cried I, what art thou doing here? On the very first onset of all this glittering clatter, thou art reduced to an atom — seek – seek some winding alley, with a tourniquet[28] at the end of it, where chariot never rolled or flambeau[29] shot its rays — there thou mayest solace thy soul in converse sweet with some kind *grisset*[30] of a barber's wife, and get into such coteries! —

— May I perish! if I do, said I, pulling out the letter which I had to present to Madame de R***. — I'll wait upon this lady, the very first thing I do. So I called La Fleur to go seek me a barber directly – and come back and brush my coat.

THE WIG

PARIS

WHEN the barber came, he absolutely refused to have anything to do with my wig: 'twas either above or below his art: I had nothing to do, but to take one ready made of his own recommendation.

—— But I fear, friend! said I, this buckle won't stand.[31] — You may immerge it, replied he, into the ocean, and it will stand —

What a great scale is everything upon in this city! thought I — The utmost stretch of an English periwig-maker's ideas could have gone no further than to have 'dipped it into a pail of water' — What difference! 'tis like time to eternity.

I confess I do hate all cold conceptions, as I do the puny ideas which engender them; and am generally so struck with the great works of nature, that for my own part, if I could help it, I never would make a comparison less than a mountain at least. All that can be said against the French sublime in this instance of it, is this – that the grandeur is *more* in the *word;* and *less* in the *thing.* No doubt the ocean fills the mind with vast ideas; but Paris being so far inland, it was not likely I should run post a hundred miles out of it, to try the experiment – the Parisian barber meant nothing. ——

The pail of water standing besides the great deep, makes certainly but a sorry figure in speech – but 'twill be said – it has one advantage – 'tis in the next room, and the truth of the buckle may be tried in it without more ado, in a single moment.

In honest truth, and upon a more candid revision of the matter, *The French expression professes more than it performs.*

I think I can see the precise and distinguishing marks of national characters more in these nonsensical *minutiæ,* than in the most important matters of state; where great men of all nations talk and stalk so much alike, that I would not give ninepence to chuse amongst them.

I was so long in getting from under my barber's hands, that it was too late of thinking of going with my letter to Madame R*** that night: but when a man is once dressed at all points for going out, his reflections turn to little account; so taking down the name of the Hotel de Modene where I lodged, I walked forth without any determination where to go — I shall consider of that, said I, as I walk along.

THE PULSE

PARIS

HAIL ye small sweet courtesies of life, for smooth do ye make the road of it! like grace and beauty which beget inclinations to love at first sight; 'tis ye who open this door and let the stranger in.

— Pray, Madame, said I, have the goodness to tell me which way I must turn to go to the Opera comique: — Most willingly, Monsieur, said she, laying aside her work —

I had given a cast with my eye into half a dozen shops as I came along in search of a face not likely to be disordered by such an interruption; till at last, this hitting my fancy, I had walked in.

She was working a pair of ruffles as she sat in a low chair on the far side of the shop facing the door —

—— *Très volontiers;* most willingly, said she, laying her work down upon a chair next her, and rising up from the low chair she was sitting in, with so chearful a movement and so chearful a look, that had I been laying out fifty louis d'ors with her, I should have said – 'This woman is grateful.'

You must turn, Monsieur, said she, going with me to the door of the shop, and pointing the way down the street I was to take – you must turn first to your left hand – *mais prenez garde* – there are two turns; and be so good as to take the second – then go down a little way and you'll see a church, and when you are past it, give yourself the trouble to turn directly to the right, and that will lead you to the foot of the *Pont Neuf*, which you must cross – and there, anyone will do himself the pleasure to shew you –

She repeated her instructions three times over to me with the same good natured patience the third time as the first; – and if *tones and manners* have a meaning, which certainly they have, unless to hearts which shut them out – she seemed really interested, that I should not lose myself.

I will not suppose it was the woman's beauty, notwithstanding she was the handsomest Grisset, I think, I ever saw, which had much to do with the sense I had of her courtesy; only I remember, when I told her how much I was obliged to her, that I looked very full in her eyes, – and that I repeated my thanks as often as she had done her instructions.

I had not got ten paces from the door, before I found I had forgot every tittle of what she had said – so looking back, and seeing her still standing in the door of the shop as if to look whether I went right or not – I returned back, to ask her whether the first turn was to my right or left – for that I had absolutely forgot. — Is it possible! said she, half laughing. — 'Tis very possible, replied I, when a man is thinking more of a woman than of her good advice.

As this was the real truth – she took it, as every woman takes a matter of right, with a slight curtsy.

— *Attendez!* said she, laying her hand upon my arm to detain me, whilst she called a lad out of the back-shop, to get ready a parcel of gloves. I am just going to send him, she said, with a packet into that quarter, and if you will have the complaisance to step in, it will be ready in a moment, and he shall attend you to the place. — So I walked in with her to the far side of the shop, and taking up the ruffle in my hand which she laid upon the chair, as if I had a mind to sit, she sat down herself in her low chair, and I instantly sat myself down besides her.

—He will be ready, Monsieur, said she, in a moment – And in that moment, replied I, most willingly would I say something very civil to you for all these courtesies. Any one may do a casual act of good nature, but a continuation of them shews it is a part of the temperature; and certainly, added I, if it is the same blood which comes from the heart, which descends to the extremes (touching her wrist) I am sure you must have one of the best pulses of any woman in the world — Feel it, said she, holding out her arm. So laying down my hat, I took of her fingers in one hand, and applied the two fore-fingers of my other to the artery. –

—Would to heaven! my dear Eugenius,[32] thou hadst passed by, and beheld me sitting in my black coat, and in my lack-a-day-sical manner, counting the throbs of it, one by one, with as much true devotion as if I had been watching the critical ebb or flow of her fever — How wouldst thou have laughed and moralized upon my new profession? – and thou shouldst have laughed and moralized on — Trust me, my dear Eugenius, I should have said, 'there are worse occupations in this world *than feeling a woman's pulse.*' — But a Grisset's! thou wouldst have said – and in an open shop! Yorick —

– So much the better: for when my views are direct, Eugenius, I care not if all the world saw me feel it.

THE HUSBAND

PARIS

I HAD counted twenty pulsations, and was going on fast towards the fortieth, when her husband coming unexpected from a back parlour into the shop, put me a little out in my reckoning. — 'Twas nobody but her husband, she said –

so I began a fresh score — Monsieur is so good, quoth she, as he passed us by, as to give himself the trouble of feeling my pulse — The husband took off his hat, and making me a bow, said, I did him too much honour – and having said that, he put on his hat and walked out.

Good God! said I to myself, as he went out – and can this man be the husband of this woman?

Let it not torment the few who know what must have been the grounds of this exclamation, if I explain it to those who do not.

In London a shopkeeper and a shopkeeper's wife seem to be one bone and one flesh: in the several endowments of mind and body, sometimes the one, sometimes the other has it, so as in general to be upon a par, and to tally with each other as nearly as man and wife need to do.

In Paris, there are scarce two orders of beings more different: for the legislative and executive powers of the shop not resting in the husband, he seldom comes there — in some dark and dismal room behind, he sits commerceless in his thrum[33] night-cap, the same rough son of Nature that Nature left him.

The genius of a people where nothing but the monarchy is *salique*,[34] having ceded this department, with sundry others, totally to the women – by a continual higgling with customers of all ranks and sizes from morning to night, like so many rough pebbles shook long together in a bag, by amicable collisions, they have worn down their asperities and sharp angles, and not only become round and smooth, but will receive, some of them, a polish like a brilliant — Monsieur *le Mari* is little better than the stone under your feet —

— Surely – surely man! it is not good for thee to sit alone – thou wast made for social intercourse and gentle greetings, and this improvement of our nature from it, I appeal to, as my evidence.

—— And how does it beat, Monsieur? said she. — With all the benignity, said I, looking quietly in her eyes, that I expected —— She was going to say something civil in return – but the lad came into the shop with the gloves — *A propos*, said I; I want a couple of pair myself.

THE GLOVES

PARIS

THE beautiful Grisset rose up when I said this, and going behind the counter, reached down a parcel and untied it: I advanced to the side over-against her: they were all too large. The beautiful Grisset measured them one by one across my hand – It would not alter the dimensions — She begged I would try a single pair, which seemed to be the least — She held it open – my hand slipped into it at once – It will not do, said I, shaking my head a little — No, said she, doing the same thing.

There are certain combined looks of simple subtlety – where whim, and sense, and seriousness, and nonsense, are so blended, that all the languages of Babel set loose together could not express them – they are communicated and caught so instantaneously, that you can scarce say which party is the infecter. I leave it to your men of words to swell pages about it – it is enough in the present to say again, the gloves would not do; so folding our hands within our arms, we both lolled upon the counter – it was narrow, and there was just room for the parcel to lay between us.

The beautiful Grisset looked sometimes at the gloves, then side-ways to the window, then at the gloves – and then at me. I was not disposed to break silence – I followed her example: so I looked at the gloves, then to the window, then at the gloves, and then at her – and so on alternately.

I found I lost considerably in every attack – she had a quick black eye, and shot through two such long and silken eye-lashes with such penetration, that she looked into my very heart and reins – It may seem strange, but I could actually feel she did —

– It is no matter, said I, taking up a couple of the pairs next me, and putting them into my pocket.

I was sensible the beautiful Grisset had not asked above a single livre above the price – I wished she had asked a livre more, and was puzzling my brains how to bring the matter about — Do you think, my dear Sir, said she, mistaking my embarrassment, that I could ask a *sous* too much of a stranger – and of a stranger whose politeness, more than his want of gloves, has done me the honour to lay himself at my mercy? – *M'en croyez capable?* – Faith! not I, said I; and if you were, you are welcome — So counting the money into her hand, and with a lower bow than one generally makes to a shopkeeper's wife, I went out, and her lad with his parcel followed me.

THE TRANSLATION

PARIS

THERE was nobody in the box I was let into but a kindly old French officer. I love the character, not only because I honour the man whose manners are softened by a profession which makes bad men worse; but that I once knew one – for he is no more – and why should I not rescue one page from violation by writing his name in it, and telling the world it was Captain Tobias Shandy,[35] the dearest of my flock and friends, whose philanthropy I never think of at this long distance from his death – but my eyes gush out with tears. For his sake, I have a predilection for the whole corps of veterans; and so I strode over the two back rows of benches, and placed myself beside him.

The old officer was reading attentively a small pamphlet, it might be the book of the opera, with a large pair of spectacles. As soon as I sat down, he took his spectacles off, and putting them into a shagreen[36] case, returned them and the book into his pocket together. I half rose up, and made him a bow.

Translate this into any civilized language in the world – the sense is this:

'Here's a poor stranger come into the box – he seems as if he knew nobody; and is never likely, was he to be seven years in Paris, if every man he comes near keeps his spectacles on his nose – 'tis shutting the door of conversation absolutely in his face – and using him worse than a German.'

The French officer might as well have said it all aloud; and if he had, I should in course have put the bow I made him into French too, and told him, 'I was sensible of his attention, and returned him a thousand thanks for it.'

There is not a secret so aiding to the progress of sociality, as to get master of this *short hand*, and be quick in rendering the several turns of looks and limbs, with all their inflections and delineations, into plain words. For my own part, by long habitude, I do it so mechanically, that when I walk the streets of London, I go translating all the way; and have more than once stood behind in the circle, where not three words have been said, and have brought off twenty different dialogues with me, which I could have fairly wrote down and sworn to.

I was going one evening to Martini's[37] concert at Milan, and was just entering the door of the hall, when the Marquesina di F***[38] was coming out in a sort of a hurry – she was almost upon me before I saw her; so I gave a spring to one side to let her pass – She had done the same, and on the same side too; so we ran our heads together: she instantly got to the other side to get out: I was just as unfortunate as she had been; for I had sprung to that side, and opposed her passage again — We both flew together to the other side, and then back — and so on — it was ridiculous; we both blushed intolerably; so I did at last the thing I should have done at first — I stood stock still, and the Marquesina had no more difficulty. I had no power to go into the room, till I had made her so much reparation as to wait and follow her with my eye to the end

of the passage — She looked back twice, and walked along
it rather side-ways, as if she would make room for anyone coming upstairs to pass her — No, said I – that's a vile
translation: the Marquesina has a right to the best apology
I can make her; and that opening is left for me to do it in
– so I ran and begged pardon for the embarrassment I had
given her, saying it was my intention to have made her way.
She answered, she was guided by the same intention towards me – so we reciprocally thanked each other. She was
at the top of the stairs; and seeing no *chichesbee*[39] near
her, I begged to hand her to her coach – so we went down
the stairs, stopping at every third step to talk of the concert and the adventure — Upon my word, Madame, said I,
when I had handed her in, I made six different efforts to
let you go out – And I made six efforts, replied she, to let
you enter — I wish to heaven you would make a seventh,
said I — With all my heart, said she, making room — Life
is too short to be long about the forms of it — so I instantly
stepped in, and she carried me home with her – And what
became of the concert, St Cecilia,[40] who, I suppose, was at
it, knows more than I.

I will only add, that the connection which arose out
of that translation, gave me more pleasure than any one I
had the honour to make in Italy.

THE DWARF

PARIS

I HAD never heard the remark made by anyone in my
life, except by one; and who that was, will probably come
out in this chapter; so that being pretty much unpre-
possessed, there must have been grounds for what struck me
the moment I cast my eyes over the *parterre* – and that was,
the unaccountable sport of nature in forming such numbers
of dwarfs — No doubt, she sports at certain times in almost every corner of the world; but in Paris, there is no

end to her amusements — The goddess seems almost as merry as she is wise.

As I carried my idea out of the *opera comique* with me, I measured everybody I saw walking in the streets by it – Melancholy application! especially where the size was extremely little – the face extremely dark – the eyes quick – the nose long – the teeth white – the jaw prominent – to see so many miserables, by force of accidents driven out of their own proper class into the very verge of another, which it gives me pain to write down – every third man a pigmy! – some by ricketty heads and hump backs – others by bandy legs – a third set arrested by the hand of Nature in the sixth and seventh years of their growth – a fourth, in their perfect and natural state, like dwarf apple-trees; from the first rudiments and stamina of their existence, never meant to grow higher.

A medical traveller might say, 'tis owing to undue bandages – a splenetic one, to want of air – and an inquisitive traveller, to fortify the system, may measure the height of their houses – the narrowness of their streets, and in how few feet square in the sixth and seventh stories such numbers of the *Bourgoisie* eat and sleep together; but I remember, Mr Shandy the elder, who accounted for nothing like anybody else, in speaking one evening of these matters, averred, that children, like other animals, might be increased almost to any size, provided they came right into the world; but the misery was, the citizens of Paris were so cooped up, that they had not actually room enough to get them — I do not call it getting anything, said he – 'tis getting nothing — Nay, continued he, rising in his argument, 'tis getting worse than nothing, when all you have got, after twenty or five and twenty years of the tenderest care and most nutritious aliment bestowed upon it, shall not at last be as high as my leg. Now, Mr Shandy being very short, there could be nothing more said upon it.

As this is not a work of reasoning, I leave the solution as I found it, and content myself with the truth only of the remark, which is verified in every lane and by-lane of Paris. I was walking down that which leads from the Carousal to the Palais Royal, and observing a little boy in some distress at the side of the gutter, which ran down the middle of it, I took hold of his hand, and helped him over. Upon turning up his face to look at him after, I perceived he was about forty – Never mind, said I; some good body will do as much for me when I am ninety.

I feel some little principles within me, which incline me to be merciful towards this poor blighted part of my species, who have neither size or strength to get on in the world – I cannot bear to see one of them trod upon; and had scarce got seated beside my old French officer, ere the disgust was exercised, by seeing the very thing happen under the box we sat in.

At the end of the orchestra, and betwixt that and the first side-box, there is a small esplanade left, where, when the house is full, numbers of all ranks take sanctuary. Though you stand, as in the parterre, you pay the same price as in the orchestra. A poor defenceless being of this order had got thrust somehow or other into this luckless place – the night was hot, and he was surrounded by beings two feet and a half higher than himself. The dwarf suffered inexpressibly on all sides; but the thing which incommoded him most, was a tall corpulent German, near seven feet high, who stood directly betwixt him and all possibility of his seeing either the stage or the actors. The poor dwarf did all he could to get a peep at what was going forwards, by seeking for some little opening betwixt the German's arm and his body, trying first one side, then the other; but the German stood square in the most unaccommodating posture that can be imagined – the dwarf might well have been placed at the bottom of the deepest draw-well in Paris; so he civilly reached up his hand to the German's sleeve, and told him his distress — The German turned his head back, looked down upon him as Goliath did upon David — and unfeelingly resumed his posture.

I was just then taking a pinch of snuff out of my monk's little horn-box — And how would thy meek and courteous spirit, my dear monk! so tempered to *bear and forbear!* – how sweetly would it have lent an ear to this poor soul's complaint!

The old French officer, seeing me lift up my eyes with an emotion, as I made the apostrophe, took the liberty to ask me what was the matter — I told him the story in three words; and added, how inhuman it was.

By this time the dwarf was driven to extremes, and in his first transports, which are generally unreasonable, had told the German he would cut off his long queue with his knife — The German looked back coolly, and told him he was welcome if he could reach it.

An injury sharpened by insult, be it to who it will, makes every man of sentiment a party: I could have leaped out of the box to have redressed it. — The old French officer did it with much less confusion; for leaning a little over, and nodding to a sentinel, and pointing at the same time with his finger at the distress – the sentinel made his way to it. — There was no occasion to tell the grievance – the thing told itself; so thrusting back the German instantly with his musket – he took the poor dwarf by the hand, and placed him before him. — This is noble! said I, clapping my hands together – And yet you would not permit this, said the old officer, in England.

— In England, dear Sir, said I, *we sit all at our ease*.

The old French officer would have set me at unity with myself, in case I had been at variance, – by saying it was a *bon mot* – and as a *bon mot* is always worth something at Paris, he offered me a pinch of snuff.

THE ROSE

PARIS

It was now my turn to ask the old French officer 'What was the matter?' for a cry of *'Haussez les mains, Monsieur l'Abbé,'* re-echoed from a dozen different parts of the parterre, was as unintelligible to me, as my apostrophe to the monk had been to him.

He told me, it was some poor Abbé in one of the upper loges, who he supposed had got planted perdu[41] behind a couple of grissets in order to see the opera, and that the parterre espying him, were insisting upon his holding up both his hands during the representation. — And can it be supposed, said I, that an ecclesiastic would pick the grissets' pockets? The old French officer smiled, and whispering in my ear, opened a door of knowledge which I had no idea of ——

Good God! said I, turning pale with astonishment – is it possible, that a people so smit with sentiment should at the same time be so unclean, and so unlike themselves — *Quelle grossierté!*[42] added I.

The French officer told me, it was an illiberal sarcasm at the church, which had begun in the theatre about the time the *Tartuffe* was given in it, by Moliere – but, like other remains of Gothic manners, was declining — Every nation, continued he, have their refinements and *grossiertés*, in which they take the lead, and lose it of one another by turns – that he had been in most countries, but never in one where he found not some delicacies, which others seemed to want. *Le* POUR *et le* CONTRE *se trouvent en chaque nation;* there is a balance, said he, of good and bad everywhere; and nothing but the knowing it is so can emancipate one half of the world from the prepossessions which it holds against the other – that the advantage of travel, as it regarded the *sçavoir vivre*, was by seeing a great deal both of men and manners; it taught us mutual toleration; and mutual toleration, concluded he, making me a bow, taught us mutual love.

The old French officer delivered this with an air of such candour and good sense, as coincided with my first favourable impressions of his character – I thought I loved the man; but I fear I mistook the object – 'twas my own way of thinking – the difference was, I could not have expressed it half so well.

It is alike troublesome to both the rider and his beast – if the latter goes pricking up his ears, and starting all the way at every object which he never saw before – I have as little torment of this kind as any creature alive; and yet I honestly confess, that many a thing gave me pain, and that I blushed at many a word the first month — which I found inconsequent and perfectly innocent the second.

Madame de Rambouliet, after an acquaintance of about six weeks with her, had done me the honour to take me in her coach about two leagues out of town — Of all women, Madame de Rambouliet is the most correct; and I never wish to see one of more virtues and purity of heart — In our return back, Madame de Rambouliet desired me to pull the cord — I asked her, if she wanted anything — *Rien que pisser*, said Madame de Rambouliet ——

Grieve not, gentle traveller, to let Madame de Rambouliet p—ss on — And ye fair mystic nymphs! go each one *pluck your rose*, and scatter them in your path – for Madame de Rambouliet did no more — I handed Madame de Rambouliet out of the coach; and had I been the priest of the chaste CASTALIA,[43] I could not have served at her fountain with a more respectful decorum.

A SENTIMENTAL JOURNEY
THROUGH
FRANCE AND ITALY

VOLUME II

A SENTIMENTAL JOURNEY
&c. &c.

THE FILLE DE CHAMBRE

PARIS

WHAT the old French officer had delivered upon travelling, bringing Polonius's advice to his son upon the same subject into my head – and that bringing in *Hamlet*; and *Hamlet*, the rest of Shakespear's works, I stopped at the Quai de Conti, in my return home, to purchase the whole set.

The bookseller said he had not a set in the world — *Comment!* said I; taking one up out of a set which lay upon the counter betwixt us. — He said, they were sent him only to be got bound, and were to be sent back to Versailles in the morning to the Count de B****.[44]

— And does the Count de B****, said I, read Shakespear? *C'est un Esprit fort*,[45] replied the bookseller. — He loves English books; and what is more to his honour, Monsieur, he loves the English too. You speak this so civilly, said I, that 'tis enough to oblige an Englishman to lay out a Louis d'or or two at your shop — the bookseller made a bow, and was going to say something, when a young decent girl of about twenty, who by her air and dress seemed to be *fille de chambre* to some devout woman of fashion, came into the shop and asked for *Les Egarements du Cœur & de l'Esprit*:[46] the bookseller gave her the book directly; she pulled out a little green sattin purse run round with a ribband of the same colour, and putting her finger and thumb into it, she took out the money, and paid for it. As I had nothing more to stay me in the shop, we both walked out at the door together.

— And what have you to do, my dear, said I, with *The Wanderings of the Heart*, who scarce know yet you have one? nor till love has first told you it, or some faithless shepherd has made it ache, can'st thou ever be sure it is so. — *Le Dieu m'en guard!* said the girl. — With reason, said I; for if it is a good one, 'tis pity it should be stolen; 'tis a little treasure to thee, and gives a better air to your face, than if it was dressed out with pearls.

The young girl listened with a submissive attention, holding her sattin purse by its ribband in her hand all the time — 'Tis a very small one, said I, taking hold of the bottom of it – she held it towards me – and there is very little in it, my dear, said I; but be but as good as thou art handsome, and heaven will fill it. I had a parcel of crowns in my hand to pay for Shakespear; and as she had let go the purse entirely, I put a single one in; and tying up the ribband in a bow-knot, returned it to her.

The young girl made me more a humble curtsy than a low one – 'twas one of those quiet, thankful sinkings, where the spirit bows itself down – the body does no more than tell it — I never gave a girl a crown in my life which gave me half the pleasure.

My advice, my dear, would not have been worth a pin to you, said I, if I had not given this along with it: but now, when you see the crown, you'll remember it – so don't, my dear, lay it out in ribbands.

Upon my word, Sir, said the girl, earnestly, I am incapable – in saying which, as is usual in little bargains of honour, she gave me her hand – *En verité, Monsieur, je mettrai cet argent apart*, said she.

When a virtuous convention is made betwixt man and woman, it sanctifies their most private walks: so notwithstanding it was dusky, yet as both our roads lay the same way, we made no scruple of walking along the Quai de Conti together.

She made me a second curtsy in setting off, and before we got twenty yards from the door, as if she had not done enough before, she made a sort of a little stop to tell me again – she thanked me.

It was a small tribute, I told her, which I could not avoid paying to virtue, and would not be mistaken in the person I had been rendering it to for the world – but I see innocence, my dear, in your face – and foul befal the man who ever lays a snare in its way!

The girl seemed affected some way or other with what I said – she gave a low sigh – I found I was not impowered to inquire at all after it – so said nothing till I got to the corner of the Rue de Nevers, where we were to part.

– But is this the way, my dear, said I, to the hotel de Modene? she told me it was – or, that I might go by the Rue de Guineygaude, which was the next turn. — Then I'll go, my dear, by the Rue de Guineygaude, said I, for two reasons; first, I shall please myself, and next, I shall give you the protection of my company as far on your way as I can. The girl was sensible I was civil – and said, she wished the hotel de Modene was in the Rue de St Pierre – You live there? said I. — She told me she was *fille de chambre* to Madame R**** — Good God! said I, 'tis the very lady for whom I have brought a letter from Amiens — The girl told me that Madame R****, she believed, expected a stranger with a letter, and was impatient to see him – so I desired the girl to present my compliments to Madame R****, and say I would certainly wait upon her in the morning.

We stood still at the corner of the Rue de Nevers whilst this passed — We then stopped a moment whilst she disposed of her *Egarements de Cœur*, &c. more commodiously than carrying them in her hand – they were two volumes; so I held the second for her whilst she put the first into her pocket; and then she held her pocket, and I put in the other after it.

'Tis sweet to feel by what fine-spun threads our affections are drawn together.

We set off afresh, and as she took her third step, the girl put her hand within my arm – I was just bidding her – but she did it of herself with that undeliberating simplicity, which shewed it was out of her head that she had never seen me before. For my own part, I felt the conviction of consanguinity so strongly, that I could not help turning half round to look in her face, and see if I could trace out anything in it of a family likeness — Tut! said I, are we not all relations?

When we arrived at the turning up of the Rue de Guineygaude, I stopped to bid her adieu for good and all: the girl would thank me again for my company and kindness — She bid me adieu twice – I repeated it as often; and so cordial was the parting between us, that had it happened anywhere else, I'm not sure but I should have signed it with a kiss of charity, as warm and holy as an apostle.

But in Paris, as none kiss each other but the men, I did what amounted to the same thing —

— I bid God bless her.

THE PASSPORT

PARIS

WHEN I got home to my hotel, La Fleur told me I had been inquired after by the Lieutenant de Police — The deuce take it! said I — I know the reason. It is time the reader should know it, for in the order of things in which it happened, it was omitted; not that it was out of my head; but that, had I told it then, it might have been forgot now — and now is the time I want it.

I had left London with so much precipitation, that it never entered my mind that we were at war with France; and had reached Dover, and looked through my glass at the hills beyond Boulogne, before the idea presented itself; and with this in its train, that there was no getting there without a passport. Go but to the end of a street, I have a mortal aversion for returning back no wiser than I set out; and as this was one of the greatest efforts I had ever made for knowledge, I could less bear the thoughts of it: so hearing the Count de **** had hired the packet, I begged he would take me in his *suite*. The Count had some little knowledge of me, so made little or no difficulty – only said, his inclination to serve me could reach no further than Calais, as he was to return by way of Brussels to Paris: however, when I had once passed there, I might get to Paris without interruption; but that in Paris I must make friends and shift for myself. — Let me get to Paris, Monsieur le Count, said I, and I shall do very well. So I embarked, and never thought more of the matter.

When La Fleur told me the Lieutenant de Police had been inquiring after me, the thing instantly recurred – and by the time La Fleur had well told me, the master of the hotel came into my room to tell me the same thing, with this addition to it, that my passport had been particularly asked after: the master of the hotel concluded with saying, He hoped I had one — Not I, faith! said I.

The master of the hotel retired three steps from me, as from an infected person, as I declared this – and poor La Fleur advanced three steps towards me, and with that sort of movement which a good soul makes to succour a distressed one – the fellow won my heart by it; and from that single *trait*, I knew his character as perfectly, and could rely upon it as firmly, as if he had served me with fidelity for seven years.

Mon seigneur! cried the master of the hotel – but recollecting himself as he made the exclamation, he instantly changed the tone of it — If Monsieur, said he, has not a passport (*apparemment*) in all likelihood he has friends in Paris who can procure him one. — Not that I know of, quoth I, with an air of indifference. — Then *certes*, replied he, you'll be sent to the Bastile or the Chatelet, *au moins*. — Poo! said I, the king of France is a good-natured soul – he'll hurt nobody. — *Cela n'empeche pas*, said he – you will certainly be sent to the Bastile to-morrow morning. — But I've taken your lodgings for a month, answered I, and I'll not quit them a day before the time for all the kings of

France in the world. La Fleur whispered in my ear, That nobody could oppose the king of France.

Pardi! said my host, *ces Messieurs Anglois sont des gens très extraordinaires* – and having both said and sworn it, he went out.

THE PASSPORT

THE HOTEL DE PARIS

I COULD not find in my heart to torture La Fleur's with a serious look upon the subject of my embarrassment, which was the reason I had treated it so cavalierly: and to shew him how light it lay upon my mind, I dropt the subject entirely; and whilst he waited upon me at supper, talked to him with more than usual gaiety about Paris, and of the opera comique. — La Fleur had been there himself, and had followed me through the streets as far as the bookseller's shop; but seeing me come out with the young *fille de chambre,* and that we walked down the Quai de Conti together, La Fleur deemed it unnecessary to follow me a step further – so making his own reflections upon it, he took a shorter cut, and got to the hotel in time to be informed of the affair of the Police against my arrival.

As soon as the honest creature had taken away, and gone down to sup himself, I then began to think a little seriously about my situation. ——

– And here I know, Eugenius, thou wilt smile at the remembrance of a short dialogue which passed betwixt us the moment I was going to set out — I must tell it here.

Eugenius, knowing that I was as little subject to be over-burthened with money as thought, had drawn me aside to interrogate me how much I had taken care for; upon telling him the exact sum, Eugenius shook his head, and said it would not do; so pulled out his purse in order to empty it into mine. — I've enough in conscience, Eugenius, said I. — Indeed, Yorick, you have not, replied Eugenius; I know

France and Italy better than you. — But you don't consider, Eugenius, said I, refusing his offer, that before I have been three days in Paris, I shall take care to say or do something or other for which I shall get clapped up into the Bastile, and that I shall live there a couple of months entirely at the king of France's expence. — I beg pardon, said Eugenius, drily; really I had forgot that resource.

Now the event I treated gaily came seriously to my door.

Is it folly, or nonchalance, or philosophy, or pertinacity – or what is it in me, that, after all, when La Fleur had gone downstairs, and I was quite alone, that I could not bring down my mind to think of it otherwise than I had then spoken of it to Eugenius?

– And as for the Bastile! the terror is in the word — Make the most of it you can, said I to myself, the Bastile is but another word for a tower – and a tower is but another word for a house you can't get out of — Mercy on the gouty! for they are in it twice a year – but with nine livres a day, and pen and ink and paper, and patience, albeit a man can't get out, he may do very well within – at least for a month or six weeks; at the end of which, if he is a harmless fellow his innocence appears, and he comes out a better and wiser man than he went in.

I had some occasion (I forget what) to step into the court-yard, as I settled this account; and remember I walked downstairs in no small triumph with the conceit of my reasoning — Beshrew the *sombre* pencil! said I, vauntingly – for I envy not its powers, which paints the evils of life with so hard and deadly a colouring: the mind sits terrified at the objects she has magnified herself and blackened; reduce them to their proper size and hue, she overlooks them — 'Tis true, said I, correcting the proposition – the Bastile is not an evil to be despised – but strip it of its towers – fill up the fossé – unbarricade the doors – call it simply a confinement, and suppose 'tis some tyrant of a distemper – and not of a man which holds you in it – the evil vanishes, and you bear the other half without complaint.

I was interrupted in the hey-day of this soliloquy, with a voice which I took to be of a child, which complained 'it could not get out.' — I looked up and down the passage, and seeing neither man, woman, or child, I went out without further attention.

In my return back through the passage, I heard the same words repeated twice over; and looking up, I saw it was a starling hung in a little cage. – 'I can't get out – I can't get out,' said the starling.

I stood looking at the bird: and to every person who came through the passage it ran fluttering to the side towards which they approached it, with the same lamentation of its captivity. — 'I can't get out,' said the starling —— God help thee! said I, but I'll let thee out, cost what it will; so I turned about the cage to get to the door; it was twisted and double twisted so fast with wire, there was no getting it open without pulling the cage to pieces – I took both hands to it.

The bird flew to the place where I was attempting his deliverance, and thrusting his head through the trellis, pressed his breast against it, as if impatient —— I fear, poor creature! said I, I cannot set thee at liberty — 'No,' said the starling — 'I can't get out – I can't get out,' said the starling.

I vow, I never had my affections more tenderly awakened; or do I remember an incident in my life, where the dissipated spirits, to which my reason had been a bubble, were so suddenly called home. Mechanical as the notes were, yet so true in tune to nature were they chanted, that in one moment they overthrew all my systematic reasonings upon the Bastile; and I heavily walked upstairs, unsaying every word I had said in going down them.

Disguise thyself as thou wilt, still slavery! said I – still thou art a bitter draught; and though thousands in all ages have been made to drink of thee, thou art no less bitter on that account. — 'Tis thou, thrice sweet and gracious goddess! addressing myself to LIBERTY, whom all in public or in private worship, whose taste is grateful, and ever wilt be so, till NATURE herself shall change – no *tint* of words can spot thy snowy mantle, or chymic power turn thy sceptre into iron – with thee to smile upon him as he eats his crust, the swain is happier than his monarch, from whose court thou art exiled — Gracious heaven! cried I, kneeling down upon the last step but one in my ascent – grant me but health, thou great Bestower of it, and give me but this fair goddess as my companion – and shower down thy mitres, if it seems good unto thy divine providence, upon those heads which are aching for them!

THE CAPTIVE

PARIS

THE bird in his cage pursued me into my room; I sat down close to my table, and leaning my head upon my hand, I begun to figure to myself the miseries of confinement. I was in a right frame for it, and so I gave full scope to my imagination.

I was going to begin with the millions of my fellow-creatures born to no inheritance but slavery; but finding, however affecting the picture was, that I could not bring it near me, and that the multitude of sad groups in it did but distract me ——

— I took a single captive, and having first shut him up in his dungeon, I then looked through the twilight of his grated door to take his picture.

I beheld his body half wasted away with long expectation and confinement, and felt what kind of sickness of the heart it was which arises from hope deferred. Upon looking nearer I saw him pale and feverish: in thirty years the western breeze had not once fanned his blood – he had seen no sun, no moon in all that time – nor had the voice of friend or kinsman breathed through his lattice – his children —

— But here my heart began to bleed – and I was forced to go on with another part of the portrait.

He was sitting upon the ground upon a little straw, in the furthest corner of his dungeon, which was alternately his chair and bed: a little calendar of small sticks were laid at the head notched all over with the dismal days and nights he had passed there – he had one of these little sticks in his hand, and with a rusty nail he was etching another day of misery to add to the heap. As I darkened the little light he had, he lifted up a hopeless eye towards the door, then cast it down, shook his head, and went on with his work of affliction. I heard his chains upon his legs, as he turned his body to lay his little stick upon the bundle — He gave a deep sigh – I saw the iron enter into his soul – I burst into tears – I could not sustain the picture of confinement which my fancy had drawn – I started up from my chair, and calling La Fleur, I bid him bespeak me a *remise*,[47] and have it ready at the door of the hotel by nine in the morning.

I'll go directly, said I, myself to Monsieur Le Duc de Choiseul.

La Fleur would have put me to bed; but not willing he should see any thing upon my cheek which would cost the honest fellow a heartache, I told him I would go to bed myself – and bid him go do the same.

THE STARLING

ROAD TO VERSAILLES

I GOT into my *remise* the hour I proposed: La Fleur got up behind, and I bid the coachman make the best of his way to Versailles.

As there was nothing in this road, or rather nothing which I look for in travelling, I cannot fill up the blank better than with a short history of this self-same bird, which became the subject of the last chapter.

Whilst the honourable Mr **** was waiting for a wind at Dover it had been caught upon the cliffs, before it could well fly, by an English lad who was his groom; who not caring to destroy it, had taken it in his breast into the packet – and by course of feeding it, and taking it once under his protection, in a day or two grew fond of it, and got it safe along with him to Paris.

At Paris the lad had laid out a livre in a little cage for the starling, and as he had little to do better the five months his master stayed there, he taught it in his mother's tongue the four simple words – (and no more) – to which I owned myself so much its debtor.

Upon his master's going on for Italy, the lad had given it to the master of the hotel – But his little song for liberty, being in an *unknown* language at Paris, the bird had little or no store set by him – so La Fleur bought both him and his cage for me for a bottle of Burgundy.

In my return from Italy I brought him with me to the country in whose language he had learned his notes – and telling the story of him to Lord A — Lord A begged the bird of me – in a week Lord A gave him to Lord B — Lord B made a present of him to Lord C – and Lord C's gentleman sold him to Lord D's for a shilling – Lord D gave him to Lord E – and so on – half round the alphabet – From that rank he passed into the lower house, and passed the hands of as many commoners – But as all these wanted to *get in* – and my bird wanted to *get out* – he had almost as little store set by him in London as in Paris.

It is impossible but many of my readers must have heard of him; and if any by mere chance have ever seen him – I beg leave to inform them, that that bird was my bird – or some vile copy set up to represent him.

I have nothing further to add upon him, but that from that time to this, I have borne this poor starling as the crest to my arms. – Thus:

—And let the herald's officers twist his neck about if they dare.

THE ADDRESS

VERSAILLES

I SHOULD not like to have my enemy take a view of my mind, when I am going to ask protection of any man: for which reason I generally endeavour to protect myself; but this going to Monsieur Le Duc de C***** was an act of compulsion—had it been an act of choice, I should have done it, I suppose, like other people.

How many mean plans of dirty address, as I went along, did my servile heart form!—I deserved the Bastile for every one of them.

Then nothing would serve me, when I got within sight of Versailles, but putting words and sentences together, and conceiving attitudes and tones to wreath myself into Monsieur Le Duc de C*****'s good graces—This will do, said

I—Just as well, retorted I again, as a coat carried up to him by an adventurous taylor, without taking his measure —Fool! continued I—see Monsieur Le Duc's face first—observe what character is written in it—take notice in what posture he stands to hear you—mark the turns and expressions of his body and limbs—And for the tone—the first sound which comes from his lips will give it you—and from all these together you'll compound an address at once upon the spot, which cannot disgust the Duke—the ingredients are his own, and most likely to go down.

Well! said I, I wish it well over—Coward again! as if man to man was not equal throughout the whole surface of the globe: and if in the field—why not face to face in the cabinet[48] too? And trust me, Yorick, whenever it is not so, man is false to himself, and betrays his own succours ten times where nature does it once. Go to the Duc de C***** with the Bastile in thy looks—my life for it, thou wilt be sent to Paris in about half an hour, with an escort.

I believe so, said I—Then I'll go to the Duke, by heaven! with all the gaiety and debonairness in the world. ——

—And there you are wrong again, replied I—A heart at ease, Yorick, flies into no extremes—'tis ever on its center.—Well! Well! cried I, as the coachman turned in at the gates, I find I shall do very well: and by the time he had wheeled round the court and brought me up to the door, I found myself so much the better for my own lecture, that I neither ascended the steps like a victim to justice, who was to part with life upon the topmost—nor did I mount them with a skip and a couple of strides, as I do when I fly up, Eliza! to thee to meet it.

As I entered the door of the saloon, I was met by a person who possibly might be the maitre d'hôtel,[49] but had more the air of one of the under secretaries, who told me the Duc de C***** was busy—I am utterly ignorant, said I, of the forms of obtaining an audience, being an absolute stranger, and what is worse in the present conjuncture of affairs, being an Englishman too.—He replied, that did not increase the difficulty.—I made him a slight bow, and told him, I had something of importance to say to Monsieur le Duc. The secretary looked towards the stairs, as if he was about to leave me to carry up this account to someone—But I must not mislead you, said I; for what I have to say is of no manner of importance to Monsieur le Duc de C*****,—but of great importance to myself. – *C'est une autre affaire*, replied he—Not at all, said I, to a man of gallantry.—But pray, good Sir, continued I, when can a stranger hope to have *accesse?*—In not less than two hours, said he, looking at his watch. The number of equipages in the court-yard seemed to justify the calculation, that I could have no nearer a prospect – and as walking backwards and forwards in the saloon, without a soul to commune with, was for the time as bad as being in the Bastile itself, I instantly went back to my *remise*, and bid the coachman drive me to the Cordon Bleu, which was the nearest hotel.

I think there is a fatality in it—I seldom go to the place I set out for.

LE PATISSER

VERSAILLES

Before I had got half-way down the street, I changed my mind: as I am at Versailles, thought I, I might as well take a view of the town; so I pulled the cord, and ordered the coachman to drive round some of the principal streets —I suppose the town is not very large, said I.—The coachman begged pardon for setting me right, and told me it was very superb, and that numbers of the first dukes and marquises and counts had hôtels—The Count de B**** of whom the bookseller at the Quai de Conti had spoke so handsomely the night before, came instantly into my mind. —And why should I not go, thought I, to the Count de B****, who has so high an idea of English books, and

Englishmen, and tell him my story? so I changed my mind a second time — In truth it was the third; for I had intended that day for Madame de R**** in the Rue St Pierre, and had devoutly sent her word by her *fille de chambre* that I would assuredly wait upon her – but I am governed by circumstances – I cannot govern them: so seeing a man standing with a basket on the other side of the street, as if he had something to sell, I bid La Fleur go up to him and inquire for the Count's hôtel.

La Fleur returned a little pale; and told me it was a Chevalier de St Louis selling *pâtés* — It is impossible, La Fleur! said I. — La Fleur could no more account for the phenomenon than myself; but persisted in his story: he had seen the croix set in gold, with its red ribband, he said, tied to his button-hole — and had looked into the basket, and seen the *pâtés* which the Chevalier was selling; so could not be mistaken in that.

Such a reverse in man's life awakens a better principle than curiosity: I could not help looking for some time at him, as I sat in the *remise* – the more I looked at him, his croix, and his basket, the stronger they wove themselves into my brain – I got out of the *remise* and went towards him.

He was begirt with a clean linen apron which fell below his knees, and with a sort of a bib that went half-way up his breast; upon the top of this, but a little below the hem, hung his croix. His basket of little pâtés was covered over with a white damask napkin; another of the same kind was spread at the bottom; and there was a look of *propreté* and neatness throughout, that one might have bought his *pâtés* of him, as much from appetite as sentiment.

He made an offer of them to neither; but stood still with them at the corner of a hôtel, for those to buy who chose it without solicitation.

He was about forty-eight – of a sedate look, something approaching to gravity. — I did not wonder. — I went up rather to the basket than him, and having lifted up the napkin, and taken one of his *pâtés* into my hand – I begged he would explain the appearance which affected me.

He told me in a few words, that the best part of his life had passed in the service, in which, after spending a small patrimony, he had obtained a company and the croix with it; but that at the conclusion of the last peace, his regiment being reformed, and the whole corps, with those of some other regiments, left without any provision, he found himself in a wide world without friends, without a livre – and indeed, said he, without any thing but this – (pointing, as he said it, to his croix) – The poor chevalier won my pity, and he finished the scene with winning my esteem too.

The king, he said, was the most generous of princes, but his generosity could neither relieve or reward every one, and it was only his misfortune to be amongst the number. He had a little wife, he said, whom he loved, who did the *patisserie;* and added, he felt no dishonour in defending her and himself from want in this way – unless Providence had offered him a better.

It would be wicked to withhold a pleasure from the good, in passing over what happened to this poor Chevalier of St Louis about nine months after.

It seems he usually took his stand near the iron gates which lead up to the palace, and as his croix had caught the eye of numbers, numbers had made the same inquiry which I had done – He had told them the same story, and always with so much modesty and good sense, that it had reached at last the king's ears – who hearing the chevalier had been a gallant officer, and respected by the whole regiment as a man of honour and integrity – he broke up his little trade by a pension of fifteen hundred livres a year.

As I have told this to please the reader, I beg he will allow me to relate another out of its order, to please myself – the two stories reflect light upon each other – and 'tis a pity they should be parted.

THE SWORD

RENNES

WHEN states and empires have their periods of declension, and feel in their turns what distress and poverty is – I stop not to tell the causes which gradually brought the house of d'E**** in Britany into decay. The Marquis d'E**** had fought up against his condition with great firmness; wishing to preserve, and still shew to the world, some little fragments of what his ancestors had been – their indiscretions had put it out of his power. There was enough left for the little exigencies of *obscurity* — But he had two boys who looked up to him for *light* – he thought they deserved it. — He had tried his sword – it could not open the way – the *mounting*[50] was too expensive – and simple œconomy was not a match for it – there was no resource but commerce.

In any other province in France, save Britany, this was smiting the root for ever of the little tree his pride and affection wished to see re-blossom — But in Britany, there being a provision for this, he availed himself of it; and taking an occasion when the states were assembled at Rennes, the Marquis, attended with his two boys, entered the court; and having pleaded the right of an ancient law of the duchy, which, though seldom claimed, he said, was no less in force; he took his sword from his side — Here, said he, take it; and be trusty guardians of it, till better times put me in condition to reclaim it.

The president accepted the Marquis's sword – he stayed a few minutes to see it deposited in the archives of his house, and departed.

The Marquis and his whole family embarked the next day for Martinico, and in about nineteen or twenty years of successful application to business, with some unlooked-for bequests from distant branches of his house — returned home to reclaim his nobility and to support it.

It was an incident of good fortune which will never happen to any traveller but a sentimental one, that I should be at Rennes at the very time of this solemn requisition: I call it solemn – it was so to me.

The Marquis entered the court with his whole family: he supported his lady – his eldest son supported his sister, and his youngest was at the other extreme of the line next his mother – he put his handkerchief to his face twice —

— There was a dead silence. When the Marquis had approached within six paces of the tribunal, he gave the Marchioness to his youngest son, and advancing three steps before his family – he reclaimed his sword. His sword was given him, and the moment he got it into his hand he drew it almost out of the scabbard – 'twas the shining face of a friend he had once given up – he looked attentively along it, beginning at the hilt, as if to see whether it was the same – when observing a little rust which it had contracted near the point, he brought it near his eye, and bending his head down over it, I think I saw a tear fall upon the place: I could not be deceived by what followed.

'I shall find,' said he, 'some *other way* to get it off.'

When the Marquis had said this, he returned his sword into its scabbard, made a bow to the guardians of it – and, with his wife and daughter and his two sons following him, walked out.

O how I envied him his feelings!

THE PASSPORT

VERSAILLES

I FOUND no difficulty in getting admittance to Monsieur le Count de B****.[51] The set of Shakespears was laid upon the table, and he was tumbling them over. I walked up close to the table, and giving first such a look at the books as to make him conceive I knew what they were, I told him I had come without anyone to present me, knowing I should meet with a friend in his apartment who, I trusted, would do it for me – It is my countryman the great Shakespear, said I, pointing to his works – *et ayez la bonté, mon cher ami*, apostrophizing his spirit, added I, *de me faire cet honneur là.* —

The Count smiled at the singularity of the introduction; and seeing I looked a little pale and sickly, insisted upon my taking an arm-chair: so I sat down; and to save him conjectures upon a visit so out of all rule, I told him simply of the incident in the bookseller's shop, and how that had impelled me rather to go to him with the story of a little embarrassment I was under, than to any other man in France — And what is your embarrassment? Let me hear it, said the Count. So I told him the story just as I have told it the reader —

— And the master of my hotel, said I, as I concluded it, will needs have it, Monsieur le Count, that I shall be sent to the Bastile – but I have no apprehensions, continued I – for in falling into the hands of the most polished people in the world, and being conscious I was a true man, and not come to spy the nakedness of the land, I scarce thought I laid at their mercy. — It does not suit the gallantry of the French, Monsieur le Count, said I, to shew it against invalids.

An animated blush came into the Count de B****'s cheeks, as I spoke this — *Ne craignez rien* — Don't fear, said he — Indeed I don't, replied I again — Besides, continued I, a little sportingly, I have come laughing all the way from London to Paris, and I do not think Monsieur le Duc de Choiseul is such an enemy to mirth, as to send me back crying for my pains.

My application to you, Monsieur le Count de B**** (making him a low bow) is to desire he will not.

The Count heard me with great good-nature, or I had not said half as much — and once or twice said – *C'est bien dit*. So I rested my cause there – and determined to say no more about it.

The Count led the discourse: we talked of indifferent things – of books and politics, and men – and then of women — God bless them all! said I, after much discourse about them – there is not a man upon earth who loves them so much as I do: after all the foibles I have seen, and all the satires I have read against them, still I love them; being firmly persuaded that a man who has not a sort of an affection for the whole sex, is incapable of ever loving a single one as he ought.

Heh bien! Monsieur l'Anglois, said the Count, gaily – You are not come to spy the nakedness of the land – I believe you – *ni encore*, I dare say, *that* of our women — But permit me to conjecture – if, *par hazard*, they fell into your way, that the prospect would not affect you.

I have something within me which cannot bear the shock of the least indecent insinuation; in the sportability of chit-chat I have often endeavoured to conquer it, and with infinite pain have hazarded a thousand things to a dozen of the sex together – the least of which I could not venture to a single one, to gain heaven.

Excuse me, Monsieur le Count, said I – as for the nakedness of your land, if I saw it, I should cast my eyes over it with tears in them — and for that of your women (blushing at the idea he had excited in me) I am so evangelical in this, and have such a fellow feeling for whatever is *weak* about them, that I would cover it with a garment, if I knew how to throw it on — But I could wish, continued I, to spy the *nakedness* of their hearts, and through the different disguises of customs, climates, and religion, find out what is good in them to fashion my own by – and therefore am I come.

It is for this reason, Monsieur le Count, continued I, that I have not seen the Palais royal – nor the Luxembourg – nor the Façade of the Louvre – nor have attempted to swell the catalogues we have of pictures, statues, and churches — I conceive every fair being as a temple, and would rather enter in, and see the original drawings and loose sketches hung up in it, than the transfiguration of Raphael itself.

The thirst of this, continued I, as impatient as that which inflames the breast of the connoisseur, has led me from my own home into France – and from France will lead me through Italy – 'tis a quiet journey of the heart in pursuit of NATURE, and those affections which arise out of her, which make us love each other – and the world, better than we do.

The Count said a great many civil things to me upon the occasion; and added very politely how much he stood obliged to Shakespear for making me known to him — But, *à-propos*, said he – Shakespear is full of great things – he forgot a small punctilio of announcing your name – it puts you under a necessity of doing it yourself.

THE PASSPORT
VERSAILLES

THERE is not a more perplexing affair in life to me, than to set about telling anyone who I am – for there is scarce anybody I cannot give a better account of than of myself; and I have often wished I could do it in a single word – and have an end of it. It was the only time and occasion in my life, I could accomplish this to any purpose – for Shakespear lying upon the table, and recollecting I was in his books, I took up *Hamlet*, and turning immediately to the grave-diggers scene in the fifth act, I laid my finger upon YORICK,[52] and advancing the book to the Count, with my finger all the way over the name — Me, *Voici!* said I.

Now whether the idea of poor Yorick's skull was put out of the Count's mind, by the reality of my own, or by what magic he could drop a period of seven or eight hundred years, makes nothing in this account – 'tis certain the French conceive better than they combine – I wonder at nothing in this world, and the less at this; inasmuch as one of the first of our own church, for whose candour and paternal sentiments I have the highest veneration, fell into the same mistake in the very same case. — 'He could not bear,' he said, 'to look into sermons wrote by the king of Denmark's jester.' — Good, my lord! said I — but there are two Yoricks. The Yorick your lordship thinks of has been dead and buried eight hundred years ago; he flourished in Horwendillus's court – the other Yorick is myself, who have flourished, my lord, in no court — He shook his head — Good God! said I, you might as well confound Alexander the Great, with Alexander the Coppersmith, my lord — 'Twas all one, he replied —

— If Alexander king of Macedon could have translated your lordship, said I, I'm sure your lordship would not have said so.

The poor Count de B**** fell but into the same *error* —

— *Et, Monsieur, est il Yorick?* cried the Count. — *Je le suis,* said I. — *Vous? – Moi – moi qui ai l'honneur de vous parler, Monsieur le Compte — Mon Dieu!* said he, embracing me — *Vous etes Yorick.*

The Count instantly put the Shakespear into his pocket, and left me alone in his room.

THE PASSPORT

VERSAILLES

I could not conceive why the Count de B**** had gone so abruptly out of the room, any more than I could conceive why he had put the Shakespear into his pocket — *Mysteries which must explain themselves are not worth the loss of time which a conjecture about them takes up:* 'twas better to read Shakespear; so taking up *Much Ado* *about Nothing*, I transported myself instantly from the chair I sat in to Messina in Sicily, and got so busy with Don Pedro and Benedick and Beatrice, that I thought not of Versailles, the Count, or the Passport.

Sweet pliability of man's spirit, that can at once surrender itself to illusions, which cheat expectation and sorrow of their weary moments! —— long – long since had ye numbered out my days, had I not trod so great a part of them upon this enchanted ground. When my way is too rough for my feet, or too steep for my strength, I get off it, to some smooth velvet path which fancy has scattered over with rose-buds of delights; and having taken a few turns in it, come back strengthened and refreshed — When evils press sore upon me, and there is no retreat from them in this world, then I take a new course — I leave it – and as I have a clearer idea of the Elysian fields than I have of heaven, I force myself, like Æneas, into them – I see him meet the pensive shade of his forsaken Dido — and wish to recognize it – I see the injured spirit wave her head, and turn off silent from the author of her miseries and dishonours – I lose the feelings for myself in hers, and in those affections which were wont·to make me mourn for her when I was at school.

Surely this is not walking in a vain shadow – nor does man disquiet himself in vain *by it* – he oftener does so in trusting the issue of his commotions to reason only. — I can safely say for myself, I was never able to conquer any one single bad sensation in my heart so decisively, as by beating up as fast as I could for some kindly and gentle sensation, to fight it upon its own ground.

When I had got to the end of the third act, the Count de B**** entered with my passport in his hand. Mons. Le Duc de C****, said the Count, is as good a prophet, I dare say, as he is a statesman — *Un homme qui rit*, said the Duke, *ne sera jamais dangereux.* — Had it been for anyone but the king's jester, added the Count, I could not have got it these two hours. —— *Pardonnez moi,*

Monsieur le Compte, said I – I am not the king's jester. — But you are Yorick? — Yes. — *Et vous plaisantez?* —— I answered, Indeed I did jest – but was not paid for it – 'twas entirely at my own expence.

We have no jester at court, Mons. le Count, said I; the last we had was in the licentious reign of Charles II — since which time our manners have been so gradually refining, that our court at present is so full of patriots, who wish for *nothing* but the honours and wealth of their country – and our ladies are all so chaste, so spotless, so good, so devout – there is nothing for a jester to make a jest of —

Voila un persiflage![53] cried the Count.

THE PASSPORT

VERSAILLES

As the passport was directed to all lieutenant-governors, governors, and commandants of cities, generals of armies, justiciaries, and all officers of justice, to let Mr Yorick, the king's jester, and his baggage, travel quietly along – I own the triumph of obtaining the passport was not a little tarnished by the figure I cut in it — But there is nothing unmixt in this world; and some of the gravest of our divines have carried it so far as to affirm that enjoyment itself was attended even with a sigh — and that the greatest *they knew of* terminated *in a general way*, in little better than a convulsion.

I remember the grave and learned Bevoriskius, in his commentary upon the generations from Adam, very naturally breaks off in the middle of a note, to give an account to the world of a couple of sparrows upon the out-edge of his window, which had incommoded him all the time he wrote, and at last had entirely taken him off from his genealogy.

— 'Tis strange! writes Bevoriskius; but the facts are

certain, for I have had the curiosity to mark them down one by one with my pen – but the cock-sparrow during the little time that I could have finished the other half this note, has actually interrupted me with the reiteration of his caresses three and twenty times and a half.

How merciful, adds Bevoriskius, is heaven to his creatures!

Ill fated Yorick! that the gravest of thy brethren should be able to write that to the world, which stains thy face with crimson, to copy in even thy study.

But this is nothing to my travels — So I twice – twice beg pardon for it.

CHARACTER

VERSAILLES

AND how do you find the French? said the Count de B****, after he had given me the passport.

The reader may suppose, that after so obliging a proof of courtesy, I could not be at a loss to say something handsome to the inquiry.

— *Mais passe, pour cela* — Speak frankly, said he; do you find all the urbanity in the French which the world give us the honour of? — I had found everything, I said, which confirmed it — *Vraiment*, said the Count. – *Les Français sont polis.* — To an excess, replied I.

The Count took notice of the world *excesse;* and would have it I meant more than I said. I defended myself a long time as well as I could against it – he insisted I had a reserve, and that I would speak my opinion frankly.

I believe, Mons. le Count, said I, that man has a certain compass, as well as an instrument; and that the social and other calls have occasion by turns for every key in him; so that if you begin a note too high or too low, there must be a want either in the upper or under part, to fill up the system of harmony. — The Count de B**** did not understand music, so desired me to explain it some other way. A polished nation, my dear Count, said I, makes every one its debtor; and besides, urbanity itself, like the fair sex, has so many charms, it goes against the heart to say it can do ill: and yet, I believe, there is but a certain line of perfection that man, take him altogether, is impowered to arrive at – if he gets beyond, he rather exchanges qualities, than gets them. I must not presume to say how far this has affected the French in the subject we are speaking of – but should it ever be the case of the English, in the progress of their refinements, to arrive at the same polish which distinguishes the French, if we did not lose the *politesse de cœur*, which inclines men more to humane actions than courteous ones – we should at least lose that distinct variety and originality of character, which distinguishes them, not only from each other, but from all the world besides.

I had a few king William's shillings as smooth as glass in my pocket; and forseeing they would be of use in the illustration of my hypothesis, I had got them into my hand, when I had proceeded so far —

See, Monsieur le Count, said I, rising up, and laying them before him upon the table – by jingling and rubbing one against another for seventy years together in one body's pocket or another's, they are become so much alike you can scarce distinguish one shilling from another.

The English, like ancient medals, kept more apart, and passing but few peoples hands, preserve the first sharpnesses which the fine hand of nature has given them – they are not so pleasant to feel – but in return, the legend is so visible, that at the first look you see whose image and superscription they bear. — But the French, Mons. le Count, added I, wishing to soften what I had said, have so many excellencies, they can the better spare this — they are a loyal, a gallant, a generous, an ingenious, and good-tempered people as is under heaven – if they have a fault – they are too *serious*.

Mon Dieu! cried the Count, rising out of his chair.

Mais vous plaisantez, said he, correcting his exclamation. — I laid my hand upon my breast, and with earnest gravity assured him it was my most settled opinion.

The Count said he was mortified, he could not stay to hear my reasons, being engaged to go that moment to dine with the Duc de C*****.

But if it is not too far to come to Versailles to eat your soup with me, I beg, before you leave France, I may have the pleasure of knowing you retract your opinion – or, in what manner you support it. — But if you do support it, Mons. Anglois, said he, you must do it with all your powers, because you have the whole world against you. — I promised the Count I would do myself the honour of dining with him before I set out for Italy – so took my leave.

THE TEMPTATION

PARIS

WHEN I alighted at the hotel, the porter told me a young woman with a band-box had been that moment inquiring for me. — I do not know, said the porter, whether she is gone or no. I took the key of my chamber of him, and went upstairs; and when I had got within ten steps of the top of the landing before my door, I met her coming easily down.

It was the fair *fille de chambre* I had walked along the Quai de Conti with: Madame de R**** had sent her upon some commissions to a *merchande de modes* within a step or two of the hotel de Modene; and as I had failed in waiting upon her, had bid her inquire if I had left Paris; and if so, whether I had not left a letter addressed to her.

As the fair *fille de chambre* was so near my door she

turned back, and went into the room with me for a moment or two whilst I wrote a card.

It was a fine still evening, in the latter end of the month of May — the crimson window-curtains (which were of the same colour of those of the bed) were drawn close – the sun was setting, and reflected through them so warm a tint into the fair *fille de chambre*'s face – I thought she blushed – the idea of it made me blush myself – we were quite alone; and that super-induced a second blush before the first could get off.

There is a sort of a pleasing half-guilty blush, where the blood is more in fault than the man – 'tis sent impetuous from the heart, and virtue flies after it – not to call it back, but to make the sensation of it more delicious to the nerves – 'tis associated. —

But I'll not describe it. — I felt something at first within me which was not in strict unison with the lesson of virtue I had given her the night before — I sought five minutes for a card – I knew I had not one —— I took up a pen – I laid it down again – my hand trembled – the devil was in me.

I know as well as anyone he is an adversary whom if we resist he will fly from us – but I seldom resist him at all; from a terror, that though I may conquer, I may still get a hurt in the combat – so I give up the triumph for security; and instead of thinking to make him fly, I generally fly myself.

The fair *fille de chambre* came close up to the bureau where I was looking for a card – took up first the pen I cast down, then offered to hold me the ink: she offered it so sweetly, I was going to accept it – but I durst not – I have nothing, my dear, said I, to write upon. – Write it, said she, simply, upon any thing. —

I was just going to cry out, Then I will write it, fair girl! upon thy lips. —

– If I do, said I, I shall perish – so I took her by the hand, and led her to the door, and begged she would not forget the lesson I had given her — She said, indeed she would not – and as she uttered it with some earnestness, she turned about, and gave me both her hands, closed together, into mine – it was impossible not to compress them in that situation – I wished to let them go; and all the time I held them, I kept arguing within myself against it – and still I held them on. — In two minutes I found I had all the battle to fight over again – and I felt my legs and every limb about me tremble at the idea.

The foot of the bed was within a yard and a half of the place where we were standing – I had still hold of her hands – and how it happened I can give no account, but I neither asked her – nor drew her – nor did I think of the bed – but so it did happen, we both sat down.

I'll just shew you, said the fair *fille de chambre*, the little purse I have been making to-day to hold your crown. So she put her hand into her right pocket, which was next me, and felt for it for some time – then into the left — 'She had lost it.' — I never bore expectation more quietly – it was in her right pocket at last – she pulled it out; it was of green taffeta, lined with a little bit of white quilted sattin, and just big enough to hold the crown – she put it into my hand – it was pretty; and I held it ten minutes with the back of my hand resting upon her lap – looking sometimes at the purse, sometimes on one side of it.

A stitch or two had broke out in the gathers of my stock[54] – the fair *fille de chambre*, without saying a word, took out her little hussive,[55] threaded a small needle, and sewed it up – I foresaw it would hazard the glory of the day; and as she passed her hand in silence across and across my neck in the manœuvre, I felt the laurels[56] shake which fancy had wreathed about my head.

A strap had given way in her walk, and the buckle of her shoe was just falling off – See, said the *fille de chambre*, holding up her foot — I could not for my soul but fasten the buckle in return, and putting in the strap – and lifting up the other foot with it, when I had done, to see both were right – in doing it too suddenly – it unavoidably threw the fair *fille de chambre* off her center – and then ——

THE CONQUEST

YES — and then — Ye whose clay-cold heads and luke-warm hearts can argue down or mask your passions, tell me, what trespass is it that man should have them? or how his spirit stands answerable to the father of spirits, but for his conduct under them?

If nature has so wove her web of kindness, that some threads of love and desire are entangled with the piece, must the whole web be rent in drawing them out? — Whip me such stoics, great governor of nature! said I to myself — Wherever thy providence shall place me for the trials of my virtue – whatever is my danger – whatever is my situation – let me feel the movements which rise out of it, and which belong to me as a man, and if I govern them as a good one, I will trust the issues to thy justice — for thou hast made us, and not we ourselves.

As I finished my address, I raised the fair *fille de chambre* up by the hand, and led her out of the room — she stood by me till I locked the door and put the key in my pocket – *and then* – the victory being quite decisive – and not till then, I pressed my lips to her cheek, and, taking her by the hand again, led her safe to the gate of the hotel.

THE MYSTERY

PARIS

IF a man knows the heart, he will know it was impossible to go back instantly to my chamber – it was touching a cold key with a flat third to it, upon the close of a piece of music, which had called forth my affections – therefore, when I let go the hand of the *fille de chambre*, I remained at the gate of the hotel for some time, looking at everyone who passed by, and forming conjectures upon them, till my attention got fixed upon a single object which confounded all kind of reasoning upon him.

It was a tall figure, of a philosophic, serious, adust[57] look, which passed and repassed sedately along the street, making a turn of about sixty paces on each side of the gate of the hotel – the man was about fifty-two – had a small cane under his arm – was dressed in a dark drab-coloured coat, waistcoat and breeches, which seemed to have seen some years service – they were still clean, and there was a little air of frugal *propreté* throughout him. By his pulling off his hat, and his attitude of accosting a good many in his way, I saw he was asking charity; so I got a sous or two out of my pocket ready to give him, as he took me in his turn – he passed by me without asking anything – and yet did not go five steps further before he asked charity of a little woman — I was much more likely to have given of the two. — He had scarce done with the woman, when he pulled off his hat to another who was coming the same way. — An ancient gentleman came slowly – and, after him, a young smart one — he let them both pass, and asked nothing: I stood observing him half an hour, in which time he had made a dozen turns backwards and forwards, and found that he invariably pursued the same plan.

There were two things very singular in this, which set my brain to work, and to no purpose – the first was, why the man should *only* tell his story to the sex – and secondly, what kind of story it was, and what species of eloquence it could be, which softened the hearts of the women, which he knew 'twas to no purpose to practise upon the men.

There were two other circumstances which entangled this mystery — the one was, he told every woman what he had to say in her ear, and in a way which had much more the air of a secret than a petition – the other was, it was always successful – he never stopped a woman, but she pulled out her purse, and immediately gave him something.

I could form no system to explain the phenomenon.

I had got a riddle to amuse me for the rest of the evening, so I walked upstairs to my chamber.

THE CASE OF CONSCIENCE

PARIS

I was immediately followed up by the master of the hotel, who came into my room to tell me I must provide lodgings elsewhere. — How so, friend? said I. – He answered, I had had a young woman locked up with me two hours that evening in my bed-chamber, and 'twas against the rules of his house. — Very well, said I, we'll all part friends then – for the girl is no worse – and I am no worse – and you will be just as I found you. — It was enough, he said, to overthrow the credit of his hotel. — *Voyez vous, Monsieur*, said he, pointing to the foot of the bed we had been sitting upon. — I own it had something of the appearance of an evidence; but my pride not suffering me to enter into any detail of the case, I exhorted him to let his soul sleep in peace, as I resolved to let mine do that night, and that I would discharge what I owed him at breakfast.

I should not have minded, *Monsieur*, said he, if you had had twenty girls — 'Tis a score more, replied I, interrupting him, than I ever reckoned upon — Provided, added he, it had been but in a morning — And does the difference of the time of the day at Paris make a difference in the sin? — It made a difference, he said, in the scandal. — I like a good distinction in my heart, and cannot say I was intolerably out of temper with the man. — I own it is necessary, re-assumed the master of the hotel, that a stranger at Paris should have the opportunities presented to him of buying lace and silk stockings and ruffles, *et tout cela* – and 'tis nothing if a woman comes with a band-box. — O' my conscience, said I, she had one; but I never looked into it. —— Then, *Monsieur*, said he, has bought nothing. —— Not one earthly thing, replied I. — Because, said he, I could recommend one to you who would use you *en conscience.*[58] — But I must see her this night, said I. – He made me a low bow and walked down.

Now shall I triumph over this *maitre d'hotel*, cried I — and what then? – Then I shall let him see I know he is a dirty fellow. — And what then? – What then! – I was too near myself to say it was for the sake of others. — I had no good answer left – there was more of spleen than principle in my project, and I was sick of it before the execution.

In a few minutes the Grisset came in with her box of lace – I'll buy nothing however, said I, within myself.

The Grisset would shew me everything – I was hard to please: she would not seem to see it; she opened her little magazine, laid all her laces one after another before me – unfolded and folded them up again one by one with the most patient sweetness – I might buy – or not – she would let me have everything at my own price – the poor creature seemed anxious to get a penny; and laid herself out to win me, and not so much in a manner which seemed artful, as in one I felt simple and caressing.

If there is not a fund of honest cullibility[59] in man, so much the worse – my heart relented, and I gave up my second resolution as quietly as the first – Why should I chastise one for the trespass of another? — If thou art tributary to this tyrant of an host, thought I, looking up in her face, so much harder is thy bread.

If I had not had more than four Louis d'ors in my purse, there was no such thing as rising up and shewing her the door, till I had first laid three of them out in a pair of ruffles.

— The master of the hotel will share the profit with

her – no matter – then I have only paid as many a poor soul has *paid* before me for an act he *could* not do, or think of.

THE RIDDLE

PARIS

WHEN La Fleur came up to wait upon me at supper, he told me how sorry the master of the hotel was for his affront to me in bidding me change my lodgings.

A man who values a good night's rest will not lie down with enmity in his heart if he can help it — So I bid La Fleur tell the master of the hotel, that I was sorry on my side for the occasion I had given him – and you may tell him, if you will, La Fleur, added I, that if the young woman should call again, I shall not see her.

This was a sacrifice not to him, but myself, having resolved, after so narrow an escape, to run no more risks, but to leave Paris, if it was possible, with all the virtue I entered in.

C'est deroger à noblesse,[60] *Monsieur*, said La Fleur, making me a bow down to the ground as he said it — *Et encore Monsieur*, said he, may change his sentiments – and if (*par hazard*) he should like to amuse himself — I find no amusement in it, said I, interrupting him —

Mon Dieu! said La Fleur – and took away.

In an hour's time he came to put me to bed, and was more than commonly officious – something hung upon his lips to say to me, or ask me, which he could not get off: I could not conceive what it was; and indeed gave myself little trouble to find it out, as I had another riddle so much more interesting upon my mind, which was that of the man's asking charity before the door of the hotel — I would have given anything to have got to the bottom of it; and that, not out of curiosity – 'tis so low a principle of inquiry, in general, I would not purchase the gratification of it with a two-sous piece – but a secret, I thought, which so soon and so certainly softened the heart of every woman you came near, was a secret at least equal to the philosopher's stone:[61] had I had both the Indies, I would have given up one to have been master of it.

I tossed and turned it almost all night long in my brains to no manner of purpose; and when I awoke in the morning, I found my spirit as much troubled with my *dreams*, as ever the king of Babylon[62] had been with his; and I will not hesitate to affirm, it would have puzzled all the wise men of Paris, as much as those of Chaldea, to have given its interpretation.

LE DIMANCHE

PARIS

It was Sunday; and when La Fleur came in, in the morning, with my coffee and roll and butter, he had got himself so gallantly arrayed, I scarce knew him.

I had covenanted at Montriul to give him a new hat with a silver button and loop, and four Louis d'ors *pour s'adoniser,*[63] when we got to Paris; and the poor fellow, to do him justice, had done wonders with it.

He had bought a bright, clean, good scarlet coat, and a pair of breeches of the same — They were not a crown worse, he said, for the wearing — I wished him hanged for telling me — They looked so fresh, that though I knew the thing could not be done, yet I would rather have imposed upon my fancy with thinking I had bought them new for the fellow, than that they had come out of the Rue de Friperie.[64]

This is a nicety which makes not the heart sore at Paris.

He had purchased moreover a handsome blue sattin waistcoat, fancifully enough embroidered – this was indeed something the worse for the service it had done, but 'twas clean scoured – the gold had been touched up, and upon the whole was rather showy than otherwise – and as the blue was not violent, it suited with the coat and breeches very well: he had squeezed out of the money, moreover, a new bag and a solitaire;[65] and had insisted with the *fripier* upon a gold pair of garters to his breeches knees — He had purchased muslin ruffles, *bien brodées*, with four livres of his own money – and a pair of white silk stockings for five more – and, to top all, nature had given him a handsome figure, without costing him a sous.

He entered the room thus set off, with his hair dressed in the first stile, and with a handsome *bouquet* in his breast – in a word, there was that look of festivity in everything about him, which at once put me in mind it was Sunday – and by combining both together, it instantly struck me, that the favour he wished to ask of me the night before, was to spend the day as everybody in Paris spent it besides. I had scarce made the conjecture, when La Fleur, with infinite humility, but with a look of trust, as if I should not refuse him, begged I would grant him the day, *pour faire le galant vis-à-vis de sa maitresse.*

Now it was the very thing I intended to do myself *vis-à-vis* Madame de R**** — I had retained the *remise* on purpose for it, and it would not have mortified my vanity to have had a servant so well dressed as La Fleur was to have got up behind it: I never could have worse spared him.

But we must *feel*, not argue in these embarrassments – the sons and daughters of service part with Liberty, but not with Nature, in their contracts; they are flesh and blood, and have their little vanities and wishes in the midst of the house of bondage, as well as their task-masters – no doubt they have set their self-denials at a price – and their expectations are so unreasonable, that I would often disappoint them, but that their condition puts it so much in my power to do it.

Behold — Behold, I am thy servant — disarms me at once of the powers of a master —

— Thou shalt go, La Fleur! said I. —

—And what mistress, La Fleur, said I, canst thou have picked up in so little a time at Paris? La Fleur laid his hand upon his breast, and said 'twas a *petite demoiselle* at Monsieur le Count de B****'s.—La Fleur had a heart made for society; and, to speak the truth of him, let as few occasions slip him as his master—so that somehow or other; but how—heaven knows—he had connected himself with the *demoiselle* upon the landing of the stair-case, during the time I was taken up with my passport; and as there was time enough for me to win the Count to my interest, La Fleur had contrived to make it do to win the maid to his —the family, it seems, was to be at Paris that day, and he had made a party with her, and two or three more of the Count's household, upon the *boulevards.*

Happy people! that once a week at least are sure to lay down all your cares together; and dance and sing, and sport away the weights of grievance, which bow down the spirit of other nations to the earth.

THE FRAGMENT

PARIS

La Fleur had left me something to amuse myself with for the day more than I had bargained for, or could have entered either into his head or mine.

He had brought the little print of butter upon a currant leaf; and as the morning was warm, and he had a good step to bring it, he had begged a sheet of waste paper to put betwixt the currant leaf and his hand—As that was plate sufficient, I bade him lay it upon the table as it was, and as I resolved to stay within all day, I ordered him to call upon the *traiteur*[66] to bespeak my dinner, and leave me to breakfast by myself.

When I had finished the butter, I threw the currant leaf out of the window, and was going to do the same by the waste paper—but stopping to read a line first, and that drawing me on to a second and third – I thought it better worth; so I shut the window, and drawing a chair up to it, I sat down to read it.

It was the old French of Rabelais's time, and for aught I know might have been wrote by him – it was moreover in a Gothic letter, and that so faded and gone off by damps and length of time, it cost me infinite trouble to make anything of it – I threw it down; and then wrote a letter to Eugenius – then I took it up again, and embroiled my patience with it afresh – and then to cure that, I wrote a letter to Eliza. — Still it kept hold of me; and the difficulty of understanding it increased but the desire.

I got my dinner; and after I had enlightened my mind with a bottle of Burgundy, I at it again – and after two or three hours poring upon it, with almost as deep attention as ever Gruter or Jacob Spon[67] did upon a nonsensical inscription, I thought I made sense of it; but to make sure of it, the best way, I imagined, was to turn it into English, and see how it would look then – so I went on leisurely, as a trifling man does, sometimes writing a sentence – then taking a turn or two – and then looking how the world went, out of the window; so that it was nine o'clock at night before I had done it – I then begun and read it as follows.

THE FRAGMENT

PARIS

——Now as the notary's wife disputed the point with the notary with too much heat – I wish, said the notary, throwing down the parchment, that there was another notary here only to set down and attest all this —

– And what would you do then, Monsieur? said she, rising hastily up – the notary's wife was a little fume of a woman, and the notary thought it well to avoid a hurricane by a mild reply – I would go, answered he, to bed. — You may go to the devil, answered the notary's wife.

Now there happening to be but one bed in the house, the other two rooms being unfurnished, as is the custom at Paris, and the notary not caring to lie in the same bed with a woman who had but that moment sent him pell-mell to the devil, went forth with his hat and cane and short cloak, the night being very windy, and walked out ill at ease towards the *Pont Neuf.*[68]

Of all the bridges which ever were built, the whole world who have passed over the *Pont Neuf* must own, that it is the noblest – the finest – the grandest – the lightest – the longest – the broadest that ever conjoined land and land together upon the face of the terraqueous globe ——

> *By this, it seems, as if the author of the fragment had not been a Frenchman.*

The worst fault which divines and the doctors of the Sorbonne can allege against it, is, that if there is but a cap-full of wind in or about Paris, 'tis more blasphemously *sacre Dieu*'d there than in any other aperture of the whole city – and with reason, good and cogent Messieurs; for it comes against you without crying *garde d'eau*,[69] and with such unpremeditable puffs, that of the few who cross it with their hats on, not one in fifty but hazards two livres and a half, which is its full worth.

The poor notary, just as he was passing by the sentry, instinctively clapped his cane to the side of it, but in raising it up, the point of his cane catching hold of the loop of the sentinel's hat, hoisted it over the spikes of the balustrade clear into the Seine ——

– *'Tis an ill wind*, said a boatsman, who catched it, *which blows nobody any good*.

The sentry, being a Gascon, incontinently twirled up his whiskers, and levelled his harquebuss.

Harquebusses in those days went off with matches; and an old woman's paper lanthorn at the end of the bridge happened to be blown out, she had borrowed the sentry's match to light it – it gave a moment's time for the Gascon's blood to run cool, and turn the accident better to his advantage — *'Tis an ill wind*, said he, catching off the notary's castor,[70] and legitimating the capture with the boatman's adage.

The poor notary crossed the bridge, and passing along the Rue de Dauphine into the fauxbourgs of St Germain, lamented himself as he walked along in this manner:

Luckless man! that I am, said the notary, to be the sport of hurricanes all my days – to be born to have the storm of ill language levelled against me and my profession wherever I go – to be forced into marriage by the thunder of the church to a tempest of a woman – to be driven forth out of my house by domestic winds, and despoiled of my castor by pontific[71] ones – to be here, bare-headed, in a windy night, at the mercy of the ebbs and flows of accidents – where am I to lay my head? – miserable man! what wind in the two-and-thirty points of the whole compass can blow unto thee, as it does to the rest of thy fellow-creatures, good!

As the notary was passing on by a dark passage, complaining in this sort, a voice called out to a girl, to bid her run for the next notary – now the notary being the next, and availing himself of his situation, walked up the passage to the door, and passing through an old sort of a saloon, was ushered into a large chamber dismantled of everything but a long military pike – a breast-plate – a rusty old sword, and bandoleer, hung up equidistant in four different places against the wall.

An old personage, who had heretofore been a gentleman, and unless decay of fortune taints the blood along with it was a gentleman at that time, lay supporting his head upon his hand in his bed; a little table with a taper burning was set close beside it, and close by the table was placed a chair – the notary sat him down in it; and pulling out his ink-horn and a sheet or two of paper which he had in his pocket, he placed them before him, and dipping his pen in his ink, and leaning his breast over the table, he disposed everything to make the gentleman's last will and testament.

Alas! Monsieur le Notaire, said the gentleman, raising himself up a little, I have nothing to bequeath which will pay the expence of bequeathing, except the history of myself, which I could not die in peace unless I left it as a legacy to the world; the profits arising out of it, I bequeath to you for the pains of taking it from me – it is a story so uncommon, it must be read by all mankind – it will make the fortunes of your house – the notary dipped his pen into his ink-horn — Almighty director of every event in my life! said the old gentleman, looking up earnestly and raising his hands towards heaven – thou whose hand has led me on through such a labyrinth of strange passages down into this scene of desolation, assist the decaying memory of an old, infirm, and broken-hearted man, direct my tongue, by the spirit of thy eternal truth, that this stranger may set down naught but what is written in that Book, from whose records, said he, clasping his hands together, I am to be condemned or acquitted! – the notary held up the point of his pen betwixt the taper and his eye ——

– It is a story, Monsieur le Notaire, said the gentleman, which will rouse up every affection in nature – it will kill the humane, and touch the heart of cruelty herself with pity ——

– The notary was inflamed with a desire to begin, and put his pen a third time into his ink-horn – and the old gentleman turning a little more towards the notary, began to dictate his story in these words ——

– And where is the rest of it, La Fleur? said I, as he just then entered the room.

THE FRAGMENT
AND THE BOUQUET*
PARIS

WHEN La Fleur came up close to the table, and was made to comprehend what I wanted, he told me there were only two other sheets of it which he had wrapt round the stalks of a *bouquet* to keep it together, which he had presented to the *demoiselle* upon the *boulevards* — Then, prithee, La Fleur, said I, step back to her to the Count de B****'s hôtel and *see if you can get it* – There is no doubt of it, said La Fleur – and away he flew.

In a very little time the poor fellow came back quite out of breath, with deeper marks of disappointment in his looks than could arise from the simple irreparability of the fragment — *Juste ciel!* in less than two minutes that the poor fellow had taken his last tender farewel of her – his faithless mistress had given his *gage d'amour* to one of the Count's footmen – the footman to a young sempstress – and the sempstress to a fidler, with my fragment at the end of it – Our misfortunes were involved together – I gave a sigh – and La Fleur echoed it back again to my ear —

– How perfidious! cried Le Fleur – How unlucky! said I. –

– I should not have been mortified, Monsieur, quoth La Fleur, if she had lost it – Nor I, La Fleur, said I, had I found it.

Whether I did or no, will be seen hereafter.

* Nosegay.

THE ACT OF CHARITY

PARIS

THE man who either disdains or fears to walk up a dark entry may be an excellent good man, and fit for a hundred things; but he will not do to make a good sentimental traveller. I count little of the many things I see pass at broad noon-day in large and open streets. — Nature is shy, and hates to act before spectators; but in such an un-observed corner, you sometimes see a single short scene of hers worth all the sentiments of a dozen French plays compounded together – and yet they are *absolutely* fine; — and whenever I have a more brilliant affair upon my hands than common, as they suit a preacher just as well as a hero, I generally make my sermon out of 'em – and for the text – 'Capadosia,[72] Pontus and Asia, Phrygia and Pamphilia' – is as good as any one in the Bible.

There is a long dark passage issuing out from the opera comique into a narrow street; 'tis trod by a few who humbly wait for a *fiacre*,* or wish to get off quietly o'foot when the opera is done. At the end of it, towards the theatre, 'tis lighted by a small candle, the light of which is almost lost before you get half-way down, but near the door – 'tis more for ornament than use: you see it as a fixed star of the least magnitude; it burns – but does little good to the world that we know of.

In returning along this passage, I discerned, as I ap-proached within five or six paces of the door, two ladies standing arm in arm, with their backs against the wall, waiting, as I imagined, for a *fiacre* — as they were next the door, I thought they had a prior right; so edged myself up within a yard or little more of them, and quietly took my stand — I was in black, and scarce seen.

The lady next me was a tall lean figure of a woman of about thirty-six; the other of the same size and make, of

* Hackney-coach.

about forty; there was no mark of wife or widow in any one part of either of them – they seemed to be two upright vestal sisters, unsapped by caresses, unbroke in upon by tender salutations: I could have wished to have made them happy – their happiness was destined, that night, to come from another quarter.

A low voice, with a good turn of expression, and sweet cadence at the end of it, begged for a twelve-sous piece betwixt them, for the love of heaven. I thought it singular, that a beggar should fix the quota of an alms – and that the sum should be twelve times as much as what is usually given in the dark. They both seemed astonished at it as much as myself. — Twelve sous! said one — A twelve-sous piece! said the other – and made no reply.

The poor man said, He knew not how to ask less of ladies of their rank, and bowed down his head to the ground.

Poo! said they, we have no money.

The beggar remained silent for a moment or two, and renewed his supplication.

Do not, my fair young ladies, said he, stop your good ears against me — Upon my word, honest man! said the younger, we have no change —— Then God bless you, said the poor man, and multiply those joys which you can give to others without change! —— I observed the elder sister put her hand into her pocket — I'll see, said she, if I have a sous. — A sous! give twelve, said the supplicant; Nature has been bountiful to you, be bountiful to a poor man.

I would, friend, with all my heart, said the younger, if I had it.

My fair charitable! said he, addressing himself to the elder — What is it but your goodness and humanity which makes your bright eyes so sweet, that they outshine the morning even in this dark passage? and what was it which made the Marquis de Santerre and his brother say so much of you both as they just passed by?

The two ladies seemed much affected; and impulsively

at the same time they both put their hands into their pocket, and each took out a twelve-sous piece.

The contest betwixt them and the poor supplicant was no more – it was continued betwixt themselves, which of the two should give the twelve-sous piece in charity – and to end the dispute, they both gave it together, and the man went away.

THE RIDDLE EXPLAINED
PARIS

I STEPPED hastily after him: it was the very man whose success in asking charity of the women before the door of the hotel had so puzzled me – and I found at once his secret, or at least the basis of it – 'twas flattery.

Delicious essence! how refreshing art thou to nature! how strongly are all its powers and all its weaknesses on thy side! how sweetly dost thou mix with the blood, and help it through the most difficult and tortuous passages to the heart!

The poor man, as he was not straitened for time, had given it here in a larger dose: 'tis certain he had a way of bringing it into less form, for the many sudden cases he had to do with in the streets; but how he contrived to correct, sweeten, concentrate, and quality it – I vex not my spirit with the inquiry – it is enough, the beggar gained two twelve-sous pieces – and they can best tell the rest, who have gained much greater matters by it.

PARIS

WE get forwards in the world not so much by doing services, as receiving them: you take a withering twig, and put it in the ground; and then you water it, because you have planted it.

Mons. le Count de B****, merely because he had done me one kindness in the affair of my passport, would go on and do me another, the few days he was at Paris, in making me known to a few people of rank; and they were to present me to others, and so on.

I had got master of my *secret* just in time to turn these honours to some little account; otherwise, as is commonly the case, I should have dined or supped a single time or two round, and then by *translating* French looks and attitudes into plain English, I should presently have seen, that I had got hold of the *couvert** of some more entertaining guest; and in course, should have resigned all my places one after another, merely upon the principle that I could not keep them. — As it was, things did not go much amiss.

I had the honour of being introduced to the old Marquis de B****:[73] in days of yore he had signalized himself by some small feats of chivalry in the *Cour d'amour*, and had dressed himself out to the idea of tilts and tournaments ever since – the Marquis de B**** wished to have it thought the affair was somewhere else than in his brain. 'He could like to take a trip to England,' and asked much of the English ladies. Stay where you are, I beseech you, Mons. le Marquis, said I —— Les Messrs. Anglois can scarce get a kind look from them as it is. — The Marquis invited me to supper.

Mons. P**** the farmer-general, was just as inquisitive about our taxes — They were very considerable, he heard — If we knew but how to collect them, said I, making him a low bow.

I could never have been invited to Mons. P****'s concerts upon any other terms.

I had been misrepresented to Madame de Q**** as an *esprit* — Madame de Q**** was an *esprit* herself; she burnt with impatience to see me, and hear me talk. I had not taken my seat, before I saw she did not care a sous whether I had any wit or no — I was let in, to be convinced she

* Plate, napkin, knife, fork, and spoon.

had. — I call heaven to witness I never once opened the door of my lips.

Madame de Q*** vowed to every creature she met, 'She had never had a more improving conversation with a man in her life.'

There are three epochas in the empire of a French woman — She is coquette – then deist – then *devôte*:[74] the empire during these is never lost – she only changes her subjects: when thirty-five years and more have unpeopled her dominions of the slaves of love, she re-peoples it with slaves of infidelity – and then with the slaves of the Church.

Madame de V***[75] was vibrating betwixt the first of these epochas: the colour of the rose was shading fast away – she ought to have been a deist five years before the time I had the honour to pay my first visit.

She placed me upon the same sopha with her, for the sake of disputing the point of religion more closely — In short, Madame de V*** told me she believed nothing.

I told Madame de V*** it might be her principle; but I was sure it could not be her interest to level the outworks, without which I could not conceive how such a citadel as hers could be defended – that there was not a more dangerous thing in the world, than for a beauty to be a deist – that it was a debt I owed my creed, not to conceal it from her – that I had not been five minutes sat upon the sopha besides her, but I had begun to form designs – and what is it, but the sentiments of religion, and the persuasion they had existed in her breast, which could have checked them as they rose up?

We are not adamant, said I, taking hold of her hand — and there is need of all restraints, till age in her own time steals in and lays them on us – but, my dear lady, said I, kissing her hand – 'tis too – too soon —

I declare I had the credit all over Paris of unperverting Madame de V***. – She affirmed to Mons. D*** and the Abbé M***,[76] that in one half hour I had said more for revealed religion, than all their Encyclopedia[77] had said against it — I was listed directly into Madame de V***'s *Coterie* – and she put off the epocha of deism for two years.

I remember it was in this *Coterie*, in the middle of a discourse, in which I was shewing the necessity of a *first cause*, that the young Count de Faineant took me by the hand to the furthest corner of the room, to tell me my *solitaire* was pinned too strait about my neck — It should be *plus badinant*,[78] said the Count, looking down upon his own – but a word, Mons. Yorick, *to the wise* –

– And from the wise, Mons. le Count, replied I, making him a bow – *is enough*.

The Count de Faineant embraced me with more ardour than ever I was embraced by mortal man.

For three weeks together, I was of every man's opinion I met. — *Pardi! ce Mons. Yorick a autant d'esprit que nous autres.* — *Il raisonne bien*, said another. —— *C'est un bon enfant*, said a third. — And at this price I could have eaten and drank and been merry all the days of my life at Paris; but 'twas a dishonest *reckoning* – I grew ashamed of it – it was the gain of a slave – every sentiment of honour revolted against it – the higher I got, the more I was forced upon my *beggarly system* – the better the *Coterie* – the more children of Art – I languished for those of Nature: and one night after a most vile prostitution of myself to half a dozen different people, I grew sick – went to bed – ordered La Fleur to get me horses in the morning to set out for Italy.

MARIA

MOULINES

I NEVER felt what the distress of plenty was in any one shape till now – to travel it through the Bourbonnois, the sweetest part of France – in the hey-day of the vintage, when Nature is pouring her abundance into everyone's lap, and every eye is lifted up – a journey through each step of which music beats time to *Labour*, and all her children are rejoicing as they carry in their clusters – to pass through this with my affections flying out, and kindling at every group before me – and every one of them was pregnant with adventures.

Just heaven! – it would fill up twenty volumes – and alas! I have but a few small pages left of this to croud it into – and half of these must be taken up with the poor Maria my friend, Mr Shandy,[79] met with near Moulines.

The story he had told of that disordered maid affected me not a little in the reading; but when I got within the neighbourhood where she lived, it returned so strong into my mind, that I could not resist an impulse which prompted me to go half a league out of the road to the village where her parents dwelt to inquire after her.

'Tis going, I own, like the Knight of the Woeful Countenance,[80] in quest of melancholy adventures – but I know not how it is, but I am never so perfectly conscious of the existence of a soul within me, as when I am entangled in them.

The old mother came to the door, her looks told me the story before she opened her mouth — She had lost her husband; he had died, she said, of anguish, for the loss of Maria's senses about a month before. — She had feared at first, she added, that it would have plundered her poor girl of what little understanding was left – but, on the contrary, it had brought her more to herself – still she could not rest – her poor daughter, she said, crying, was wandering somewhere about the road —

— Why does my pulse beat languid as I write this? and what made La Fleur, whose heart seemed only to be tuned to joy, to pass the back of his hand twice across his eyes, as the woman stood and told it? I beckoned to the postillion to turn back into the road.

When we had got within half a league of Moulines, at a little opening in the road leading to a thicket, I discovered poor Maria sitting under a poplar — she was sitting with her elbow in her lap, and her head leaning on one side within her hand – a small brook ran at the foot of the tree.

I bid the postillion go on with the chaise to Moulines – and La Fleur to bespeak my supper – and that I would walk after him.

She was dressed in white, and much as my friend described her, except that her hair hung loose, which before was twisted within a silk net. — She had, superadded likewise to her jacket, a pale green ribband which fell across her shoulder to the waist; at the end of which hung her pipe. — Her goat had been as faithless as her lover; and she had got a little dog in lieu of him, which she had kept tied by a string to her girdle; as I looked at her dog, she drew him towards her with the string. — 'Thou shalt not leave me, Sylvio,' said she. I looked in Maria's eyes, and saw she was thinking more of her father than of her lover or her little goat; for as she uttered them the tears trickled down her cheeks.

I sat down close by her; and Maria let me wipe them away as they fell with my handkerchief — I then steeped it in my own – and then in hers – and then in mine – and then I wiped hers again – and as I did it, I felt such undescribable emotions within me, as I am sure could not be accounted for from any combinations of matter and motion.

I am positive I have a soul; nor can all the books with which materialists have pestered the world ever convince me of the contrary.

MARIA

WHEN Maria had come a little to herself, I asked her if she remembered a pale thin person of a man who had sat down betwixt her and her goat about two years before? She said, she was unsettled much at that time, but remembered it upon two accounts – that ill as she was she saw the person pitied her; and next, that her goat had stolen his handkerchief, and she had beat him for the theft – she had washed it, she said, in the brook, and kept it ever since in her pocket to restore it to him in case she should ever see him again, which, she added, he had half promised her. As she told me this she took the handkerchief out of her pocket to let me see it; she had folded it up neatly in a couple of vine leaves, tied round with a tendril – on opening it, I saw an S marked in one of the corners.

She had since that, she told me, strayed as far as Rome, and walked round St Peter's once – and returned back – that she found her way alone across the Apennines – had travelled over all Lombardy without money – and through the flinty roads of Savoy without shoes – how she had borne it, and how she had got supported, she could not tell – but *God tempers the wind*, said Maria, to the shorn lamb.

Shorn indeed! and to the quick, said I; and wast thou in my own land, where I have a cottage, I would take thee to it and shelter thee: thou shouldst eat of my own bread, and drink of my own cup — I would be kind to thy Sylvio – in all thy weaknesses and wanderings I would seek after thee and bring thee back – when the sun went down I would say my prayers, and when I had done thou shouldst play thy evening song upon thy pipe; nor would the incense of my sacrifice be worse accepted for entering heaven along with that of a broken heart.

Nature melted within me, as I uttered this; and Maria observing, as I took out my handkerchief, that it was steeped too much already to be of use, would needs go wash it in the stream. — And where will you dry it, Maria? said I — I'll dry it in my bosom, said she — 'twill do me good.

And is your heart still so warm, Maria? said I.

I touched upon the string on which hung all her sorrows – she looked with wistful disorder for some time in my face; and then, without saying anything, took her pipe, and played her service to the Virgin — The string I had touched ceased to vibrate – in a moment or two Maria returned to herself – let her pipe fall – and rose up.

And where are you going, Maria? said I. — She said to Moulines. — Let us go, said I, together. — Maria put her arm within mine, and lengthening the string, to let the dog follow, in that order we entered Moulines.

MARIA

MOULINES

THOUGH I hate salutations and greetings in the market-place, yet when we got into the middle of this, I stopped to take my last look and last farewel of Maria.

Maria, though not tall, was nevertheless of the first order of fine forms – affliction had touch'd her looks with something that was scarce earthly – still she was feminine – and so much was there about her of all that the heart wishes, or the eye looks for in woman, that could the traces be ever worn out of her brain, and those of Eliza's out of mine, she should *not only eat of my bread and drink of my own cup*, but Maria should lay in my bosom, and be unto me as a daughter.

Adieu, poor luckless maiden! — imbibe the oil and wine which the compassion of a stranger, as he journeyeth on his way, now pours into thy wounds – the being who has twice bruised thee can only bind them up for ever.

THE BOURBONNOIS

THERE was nothing from which I had painted out for myself so joyous a riot of the affections, as in this journey in the vintage, through this part of France; but pressing through this gate of sorrow to it, my sufferings had totally unfitted me: in every scene of festivity I saw Maria in the background of the piece, sitting pensive under her poplar; and I had got almost to Lyons before I was able to cast a shade across her —

— Dear sensibility! source inexhausted of all that's precious in our joys, or costly in our sorrows! thou chainest thy martyr down upon his bed of straw – and 'tis thou who lifts him up to HEAVEN – eternal fountain of our feelings! – 'tis here I trace thee — and this is thy divinity which stirs within me — not that, in some sad and sickening moments, *my soul shrinks back upon herself, and startles at destruction* — mere pomp of words! — but that I feel some generous joys and generous cares beyond myself – all comes from thee, great, great SENSORIUM of the world! which vibrates, if a hair of our heads but falls upon the ground, in the remotest desert of thy creation. — Touched with thee, Eugenius draws my curtain when I languish – hears my tale of symptoms, and blames the weather for the disorder of his nerves. Thou givest a portion of it sometimes to the roughest peasant who traverses the bleakest mountains – he finds the lacerated lamb of another's flock — This moment I behold him leaning with his head against his crook, with piteous inclination looking down upon it! — Oh! had I come one moment sooner! — it bleeds to death — his gentle heart bleeds with it ——

Peace to thee, generous swain! — I see thou walkest off with anguish – but thy joys shall balance it – for happy is thy cottage – and happy is the sharer of it – and happy are the lambs which sport about you.

THE SUPPER

A SHOE coming loose from the fore-foot of the thill-horse, at the beginning of the ascent of mount Taurira, the postillion dismounted, twisted the shoe off, and put it in his pocket; as the ascent was of five or six miles, and that horse our main dependence, I made a point of having the shoe fastened on again, as well as we could; but the postillion had thrown away the nails, and the hammer in the chaise-box being of no great use without them, I submitted to go on.

He had not mounted half a mile higher, when coming to a flinty piece of road, the poor devil lost a second shoe, and from off his other fore-foot; I then got out of the chaise in good earnest; and seeing a house about a quarter of a mile to the left-hand, with a great deal to do I prevailed upon the postillion to turn up to it. The look of the house, and of everything about it, as we drew nearer, soon reconciled me to the disaster. — It was a little farmhouse surrounded with about twenty acres of vineyard, about as much corn – and close to the house, on one side, was a *potagerie*[81] of an acre and a half, full of everything which could make plenty in a French peasant's house – and on the other side was a little wood which furnished wherewithal to dress it. It was about eight in the evening when I got to the house – so I left the postillion to manage his point as he could – and for mine, I walked directly into the house.

The family consisted of an old grey-headed man and his wife, with five or six sons and sons-in-law, and their several wives, and a joyous genealogy out of 'em.

They were all sitting down together to their lentil-soup; a large wheaten loaf was in the middle of the table; and a flaggon of wine at each end of it promised joy through the stages of the repast – 'twas a feast of love.

The old man rose up to meet me, and with a respectful cordiality would have me sit down at the table; my heart was sat down the moment I entered the room; so I sat down at once like a son of the family; and to invest myself in the character as speedily as I could, I instantly borrowed the old man's knife, and taking up the loaf, cut myself a hearty luncheon; and as I did it, I saw a testimony in every eye, not only of an honest welcome, but of a welcome mixed with thanks that I had not seemed to doubt it.

Was it this; or tell me, Nature, what else it was which

made this morsel so sweet – and to what magic I owe it, that the draught I took of their flaggon was so delicious with it, that they remain upon my palate to this hour?

If the supper was to my taste – the grace that followed it was much more so.

THE GRACE

WHEN supper was over, the old man gave a knock upon the table with the haft of his knife — to bid them prepare for the dance: the moment the signal was given, the women and girls ran all together into a back apartment to tie up their hair – and the young men to the door to wash their faces, and change their sabots;[82] and in three minutes every soul was ready upon a little esplanade before the house to begin — The old man and his wife came out last, and, placing me betwixt them, sat down upon a sopha of turf by the door.

The old man had some fifty years ago been no mean performer upon the vielle[83] – and, at the age he was then of, touched it well enough for the purpose. His wife sung now and then a little to the tune – then intermitted – and joined her old man again as their children and grand-children danced before them.

It was not till the middle of the second dance, when, from some pauses in the movement wherein they all seemed to look up, I fancied I could distinguish an eleva-tion of spirit different from that which is the cause or the effect of simple jollity — In a word, I thought I beheld *Religion* mixing in the dance – but as I had never seen her so engaged, I should have looked upon it now, as one of the illusions of an imagination which is eternally misleading me, had not the old man, as soon as the dance ended, said, that this was their constant way; and that all his life long he had made it a rule, after supper was over, to call out his family to dance and rejoice; believing, he said, that a chearful and contented mind was the best sort of thanks to heaven that an illiterate peasant could pay —

— Or a learned prelate either, said I.

THE CASE OF DELICACY[84]

WHEN you have gained the top of mount Taurira, you run presently down to Lyons – adieu then to all rapid movements! 'Tis a journey of caution; and it fares better with sentiments, not to be in a hurry with them; so I contracted with a voiturin[85] to take his time with a couple of mules, and convey me in my own chaise safe to Turin through Savoy.

Poor, patient, quiet, honest people! fear not; your poverty, the treasury of your simple virtues, will not be envied you by the world, nor will your valleys be invaded by it. — Nature! in the midst of thy disorders, thou art still friendly to the scantiness thou hast created – with all thy great works about thee, little hast thou left to give, either to the scithe or to the sickle – but to that little thou grantest safety and protection; and sweet are the dwellings which stand so sheltered.

Let the way-worn traveller vent his complaints upon the sudden turns and dangers of your roads – your rocks – your precipices – the difficulties of getting up – the horrors of getting down – mountains impracticable – and cataracts, which roll down great stones from their summits, and block up his road. — The peasants had been all day at work in removing a fragment of this kind between St Michael and Madane; and by the time my voiturin got to the place, it wanted full two hours of completing before a passage could any how be gained: there was nothing but to wait with patience – 'twas a wet and tempestuous night; so that by the delay, and that together, the voiturin found himself obliged to take up five miles short of his stage at a little decent kind of an inn, by the road side.

I forthwith took possession of my bed-chamber – got a good fire – ordered supper; and was thanking heaven it was no worse – when a voiture arrived with a lady in it and her servant-maid.

As there was no other bed-chamber in the house, the hostess, without much nicety, led them into mine, telling them as she ushered them in, that there was nobody in it but an English gentleman – that there were two good beds in it, and a closet within the room which held another – the accent in which she spoke of this third bed did not say much for it – however, she said, there were three beds, and but three people – and she durst say, the gentleman would do anything to accommodate matters. — I left not the lady a moment to make a conjecture about it – so instantly made a declaration I would do anything in my power.

As this did not amount to an absolute surrender of my bed-chamber. I still felt myself so much the proprietor, as to have a right to do the honours of it – so I desired the lady to sit down – pressed her into the warmest seat – called for more wood – desired the hostess to enlarge the plan of the supper, and to favour us with the very best wine.

The lady had scarce warmed herself five minutes at the fire, before she began to turn her head back, and give a look at the beds; and the oftener she cast her eyes that way, the more they returned perplexed — I felt for her – and for myself; for in a few minutes, what by her looks, and the case itself, I found myself as much embarrassed as it was possible the lady could be herself.

That the beds we were to lay in were in one and the same room, was enough simply by itself to have excited all this – but the position of them, for they stood parallel, and so very close to each other as only to allow space for a small wicker chair betwixt them, rendered the affair still more oppressive to us – they were fixed up moreover near the fire, and the projection of the chimney on one side, and a large beam which crossed the room on the other, formed a kind of recess for them that was no way favourable to the nicety of our sensations – if anything could have added to it, it was, that the two beds were both of 'em so very small, as to cut us off from every idea of the lady and the maid lying together; which in either of them, could it have been feasible, my lying besides them, though a thing not to be wished, yet there was nothing in it so terrible which the imagination might not have passed over without torment.

As for the little room within, it offered little or no consolation to us; 'twas a damp cold closet, with a half-dismantled window-shutter, and with a window which had neither glass or oil-paper in it to keep out the tempest of the night. I did not endeavour to stifle my cough when the lady gave a peep into it; so it reduced the case in course to this alternative – that the lady should sacrifice her health to her feelings, and take up with the closet herself, and abandon the bed next mine to her maid – or that the girl should take the closet, &c. &c.

The lady was a Piedmontese of about thirty, with a glow of health in her cheeks: the maid was a Lyonoise of twenty, and as brisk and lively a French girl as ever moved. — There were difficulties every way – and the obstacle of the stone in the road, which brought us into the distress, great as it appeared whilst the peasants were removing it, was but a pebble to what lay in our ways now — I have only to add, that it did not lessen the weight which hung upon our spirits, that we were both too delicate to communicate what we felt to each other upon the occasion.

We sat down to supper; and had we not had more generous wine to it than a little inn in Savoy could have furnished, our tongues had been tied up, till necessity herself had set them at liberty — but the lady having a few bottles of Burgundy in her voiture sent down her fille de chambre for a couple of them; so that by the time supper was over, and we were left alone, we felt ourselves inspired with a strength of mind sufficient to talk, at least, without reserve upon our situation. We turned it every way, and debated and considered it in all kind of lights in the course of a two hours negociation; at the end of which the articles were settled finally betwixt us, and stipulated for in form and manner of a treaty of peace – and I believe with as much religion and good faith on both sides, as in any treaty which as yet had the honour of being handed down to posterity.

They were as follow:

First. As the right of the bed-chamber is in Monsieur, and he thinking the bed next to the fire to be the warmest, he insists upon the concession on the lady's side of taking up with it.

Granted, on the part of Madame; with a proviso, That as the curtains of that bed are of a flimsy transparent cotton, and appear likewise too scanty to draw close, that the fille de chambre shall fasten up the opening, either by corking pins,[86] or needle and thread, in such manner as shall be deemed a sufficient barrier on the side of Monsieur.

2dly. It is required on the part of Madame, that Monsieur shall lay the whole night through in his robe de chambre.

Rejected: inasmuch as Monsieur is not worth a robe de chambre; he having nothing in his portmanteau but six shirts and a black silk pair of breeches.

The mentioning the silk pair of breeches made an entire change of the article – for the breeches were accepted as an equivalent for the robe de chambre; and so it was stipulated and agreed upon that I should lie in my black silk breeches all night.

3dly. It was insisted upon, and stipulated for by the lady, that after Monsieur was got to bed, and the candle and fire extinguished, that Monsieur should not speak one single word the whole night.

Granted; provided Monsieur's saying his prayers might not be deemed an infraction of the treaty.

There was but one point forgot in this treaty, and that

was the manner in which the lady and myself should be obliged to undress and get to bed – there was but one way of doing it, and that I leave to the reader to devise; protesting as I do it, that if it is not the most delicate in nature, 'tis the fault of his own imagination – against which this is not my first complaint.

Now when we were got to bed, whether it was the novelty of the situation, or what it was, I know not, but so it was, I could not shut my eyes; I tried this side and that, and turned and turned again, till a full hour after midnight, when nature and patience both wearing out – O my God! said I —

— You have broke the treaty, Monsieur, said the lady, who had no more slept than myself. — I begged a thousand pardons – but insisted it was no more than an ejaculation – she maintained 'twas an entire infraction of the treaty — I maintained it was provided for in the clause of the third article.

The lady would by no means give up her point, though she weakened her barrier by it; for in the warmth of the dispute, I could hear two or three corking pins fall out of the curtain to the ground.

Upon my word and honour, Madame, said I – stretching my arm out of bed by way of asseveration —

— (I was going to have added, that I would not have trespassed against the remotest idea of decorum for the world) —

— But the fille de chambre hearing there were words between us, and fearing that hostilities would ensue in course, had crept silently out of her closet, and it being totally dark, had stolen so close to our beds, that she had got herself into the narrow passage which separated them, and had advanced so far up as to be in a line betwixt her mistress and me —

So that when I stretched out my hand, I caught hold of the fille de chambre's —

END

NOTES

1. (p. 27) *Eliza*: Mrs Elizabeth Draper, the young wife of an official of the East India Company in Bombay, whom Sterne met in 1767, and with whom he conducted a Platonic and 'sentimental' friendship, in person and by correspondence, until shortly before his death. The *Journal to Eliza* reveals, in a relatively crude form, the kind of emotionalism which is refined and polished into art in *A Sentimental Journey*.

2. (p. 28) *precieuse*: originally meant a woman of culture and refinement; after Molière's *Les Précieuses ridicules* (1659), it came to mean an ignorant and stupid woman aping these things.

3. (p. 29) *Guido*: Guido Reni (1575–1642), Italian painter.

4. (p. 32) *Monsieur Dessein*: Pierre Quillacq, *dit* Dessin, the innkeeper, became one of the richest men in Calais merely by being mentioned in *A Sentimental Journey*. He assured an American visitor to Calais in 1776 that Father Lorenzo, the monk, had never existed (*The American Wanderer through Various Parts of Europe, by a Virginian*, Dublin, 1783, p. 145).

5. (p. 33) *efficient* cause: that which makes a thing to be what it is.

   final cause: the end or purpose for which a thing is done, viewed as a cause of the act.

6. (p. 34) *peregrine*: foreign, imported from abroad.

7. (p. 37) *Vis a Vis*: carriage in which persons sit facing each other.

8. (p. 38) *Remise*: coach-house.

9. (p. 39) *diabled*: i.e. cursed.

10. (p. 41) *Esdras*: the reputed author of two books of the Apocrypha. The quotation comes from II Esdras x. 31, and the words are those of an angel speaking to the prophet. This book is a record of angelic visitations, prophesying the salvation of the righteous and the destruction of the wicked.

11. (p. 46) *tartufish*: 'hypocritical', from the central character of Molière's *Tartuffe* (1664).

12. (p. 51) *from Dan to Beersheba*: i.e. from one end of the country to the other. Dan was at the extreme north of the land

of Canaan; Beersheba at the extreme south. The phrase is used literally in Judges xx. 1; Sterne seems to have been the first to use it in a figurative sense.

13. (p. 51) *Smelfungus*: Sterne's name for the novelist Tobias Smollett, whose *Travels Through France and Italy* had been published in 1766. His book is full of complaints about these countries and their inhabitants, and he comments that the Pantheon looks 'like a huge cockpit, open at the top', while the Venus de Medici 'has no beauty in the features' and 'the attitude is awkward and out of character'. Sterne certainly did not meet him in Italy in 1766, as he implies here; they may have met in Montpellier in 1763.

14. (p. 52) *'wherein he spoke . . . Anthropophagi'*: *Othello* I. 3. 134–44:

> Wherein I spake of most disastrous chances,
> Of moving accidents by flood and field,
>
> . . .
>
> And of the Cannibals that each other eat,
> The Anthropophagi. . . .

15. (p. 52) *St Bartholomew*: one of the twelve apostles. He is said to have preached in Asia Minor and north-west India, and to have been flayed alive.

16. (p. 52) *Mundungus*: Sterne's name for Dr Samuel Sharp, who published *Letters from Italy* in 1766.

17. (p. 54) *H—*: David Hume, the philosopher and historian, secretary to the English ambassador in Paris from 1763 to 1765. Sterne met him in Paris in 1764 and became very friendly with him. John Home (1722–1808) was the author of the tragedy *Douglas*, first produced in 1756 and extremely popular at the time. The two names were pronounced alike.

18. (p. 55) *spatterdashes*: leggings to protect stockings etc. from mud and dirt.

19. (p. 55) *La Fleur*: Sterne may have taken the name for his valet from a character in *Le Glorieux* (1732), a play by Philippe Néricault-Destouches. In the play he is a lackey who is miserable because his master is too proud to speak to him. An account of Sterne's journey, purporting to be taken verbatim from La Fleur himself, appeared in the *European Magazine* in 1790.

20. (p. 57) *Abdera*: a Greek city on the coast of Thrace, whose inhabitants were proverbial for stupidity. The philosopher Democritus, known as 'the laughing philosopher' for his attempt to laugh men out of their follies, was born there about 460 B.C. The *Andromeda* is one of the lost plays of Euripides, and survives only in fragments, such as the one Sterne gives here.

21. (p. 57) *pasquinades*: lampoons or satires fixed in a public place.

22. (p. 58) *helebore*: 'hellebore' is the ancient name of various plants supposed to cure madness.

23. (p. 61) *doublets*: the same number on two dice thrown at once.

24. (p. 62) *cast*: fortune, fate.

25. (p. 67) *prevenancy*: obliging manner, complaisance.

26. (p. 68) *etourderie*: blunder, thoughtlessness.

27. (p. 71) *signalize*: make noteworthy or remarkable.
    cabinet: i.e. in politics.

28. (p. 71) *tourniquet*: turnstile.

29. (p. 71) *flambeau*: torch, especially one made of several thick wicks dipped in wax.

30. (p. 71) *grisset*: or 'grisette', a French girl or young woman of the working class; usually applied to a shop assistant or seamstress.

31. (p. 72) *stand*: hold together, resist wear or damage.

32. (p. 75) *Eugenius*: Sterne's name for his lifelong friend John Hall-Stevenson.

33. (p. 76) *thrum*: made of thrums or waste threads of yarn.

34. (p. 76) *salique*: the French monarchy was allegedly based on the Salic law of Merovingian times, which excluded females from dynastic succession.

35. (p. 78) *Captain Tobias Shandy*: 'Uncle Toby' of Sterne's *Tristram Shandy*.

36. (p. 78) *shagreen*: species of untanned leather with an artificially granulated surface, made from the skin of horse, ass, camel, seal etc. and usually dyed green.

37. (p. 79) *Martini*: probably Giovanni Battista Martini (1706–86), a composer who was also the finest music teacher and theorist of his time.

38. (p. 79) *Marquesina di F****: this refers to an actual en-

counter between Sterne and the Marchesa Fagniani in Milan in 1765.

39. (p. 80) *chichesbee*: form of 'cicisbeo', the name formerly given in Italy to the 'cavalier servente' or recognized gallant of a married woman.

40. (p. 80) *St Cecilia*: the patron saint of church music.

41. (p. 84) *perdu*: hidden.

42. (p. 84) *grossierté*: coarseness, vulgarity.

43. (p. 85) *Castalia*: the daughter of Achelous, who plunged into a spring on Mount Parnassus to escape from Apollo. The spring was named after her and became sacred to Apollo and the Muses.

44. (p. 89) *Count de B*****: the Comte de Bissy, whom Sterne met in Paris in 1762.

45. (p. 89) *Esprit fort*: a wit; someone who expresses superiority to current prejudices.

46. (p. 89) *Les Egarements du Cœur & de l'Esprit*: a novel by Crébillon *fils*, whom Sterne also met in Paris in 1762.

47. (p. 98) *remise*: carriage hired from a livery-stable.

48. (p. 101) *cabinet*: small private room.

49. (p. 101) *maitre d'hôtel*: steward, butler. The French word 'hôtel' means a large private residence or town mansion (e.g. on p. 102, line 28). During the 1760s, however, the word 'hotel' was coming into common use in English as a term for a superior kind of inn. Sterne uses both words frequently in *A Sentimental Journey*.

50. (p. 105) *mounting*: soldier's outfit or equipment.

51. (p. 106) *le Count de B*****: the characters and incidents of this section of the book are based on Sterne's first visit to Paris in 1762, rather than on the visit to France and Italy in 1765–6 which forms the basis for most of the other incidents. When Sterne arrived in Paris in 1762, the Comte de Bissy helped him to obtain a passport from the Duc de Choiseul, the prime minister. When Sterne first visited the Comte, he was flattered to find a copy of *Tristram Shandy* open on his table.

52. (p. 109) *Yorick*: Sterne had introduced the character Parson Yorick into *Tristram Shandy*, and when he published his own first collection of sermons he entitled them *The Sermons of Mr Yorick*. The title drew many objections from reviewers

and clergymen. In *A Sentimental Journey* he of course adopts the pseudonym Yorick for himself.

53. (p. 112) *persiflage*: banter, jest.

54. (p. 117) *the gathers of my stock*: the 'gathers' are that part of an article of dress which is gathered, or drawn in. The 'stock' was a stiff wide band of leather, linen, or other material formerly worn round the neck.

55. (p. 117) *hussive*: from 'housewife', a case for needles, thread etc.

56. (p. 117) *laurels*: awarded for his 'victory' in his battle for self-control.

57. (p. 119) *adust*: gloomy.

58. (p. 121) *en conscience*: in good faith, conscientiously.

59. (p. 121) *cullibility*: gullibility.

60. (p. 122) *deroger à noblesse*: to lose caste, make oneself cheap.

61. (p. 123) *the philosopher's stone*: substance supposed to change other metals into gold or silver.

62. (p. 123) *the king of Babylon*: Nebuchadnezzar, whose dreams were interpreted by Daniel.

63. (p. 123) *s'adoniser*: to smarten oneself up.

64. (p. 123) *Rue de Friperie*: a 'friperie' is a shop selling second-hand clothes.

65. (p. 124) *a new bag*: a small silken pouch to contain the back-hair of a wig.

solitaire: a loose neck-tie of black silk or broad ribbon.

66. (p. 125) *traiteur*: keeper of an eating-house.

67. (p. 126) *Gruter or Jacob Spon*: Jan Gruytère (1560–1627) was a Dutch classical scholar. Jacob Spon (1647–85) was a French antiquary and physician.

68. (p. 127) *Pont Neuf*: the oldest bridge in Paris, built between 1578 and 1604.

69. (p. 127) *garde d'eau*: a warning cry uttered (in eighteenth-century Edinburgh – usually in the form of 'gardyloo') before throwing dirty water etc. from the window into the street.

70. (p. 128) *castor*: a hat, originally made of beaver's fur, but by the eighteenth century usually made from rabbit's fur.

71. (p. 128) *pontific*: a humorous coinage of Sterne's own, meaning 'pertaining to a bridge'.

72. (p. 131) *Capadosia*: i.e. Cappadocia, a region of eastern Asia Minor.

73. (p. 134) *Marquis de B*****: the Duc de Biron, whom, like M. La Popelinière ('Mons. P****') the farmer-general (tax-gatherer), Sterne met in Paris in 1762.

74. (p. 135) *devôte*: extremely devout woman.

75. (p. 135) *Madame de V****: Madame de Vence, another of Sterne's Paris acquaintances of 1762.

76. (p. 135) *Mons. D*** and the Abbé M****: Denis Diderot, the writer, and the Abbé Morellet.

77. (p. 135) *Encyclopedia*: published under the direction of Diderot and d'Alembert between 1751 and 1776, and including articles by Voltaire, Montesquieu, and Rousseau, the *Encyclopédie* was the embodiment of the rationalistic spirit of the eighteenth century, and its sceptical tendencies brought it under frequent attack from the clergy.

78. (p. 136) *badinant*: jesting, trifling.

79. (p. 137) *Mr Shandy*: Sterne told the story of Maria of Moulines twice in print: once in the ninth volume of *Tristram Shandy*, published in 1767, and again in *A Sentimental Journey* in 1768. The incident which formed the basis of the story must have occurred during his journey through France in 1765.

80. (p. 137) *the Knight of the Woeful Countenance*: i.e. Don Quixote.

81. (p. 142) *potagerie*: a kitchen-garden.

82. (p. 143) *sabots*: shoe hollowed out from one piece of wood, worn by the French lower classes.

83. (p. 143) *vielle*: a musical instrument with four strings played by means of a small wheel.

84. (p. 144) *The Case of Delicacy*: this incident is based on an adventure which happened to John Craufurd of Errol, a young gentleman whom Sterne met in Paris in 1765.

85. (p. 144) *voiturin*: the driver of a carriage or coach. It can also be used for the carriage itself.

86. (p. 147) *corking pins*: pins of the largest size.

FOR THE BEST IN PAPERBACKS, LOOK FOR THE

In every corner of the world, on every subject under the sun, Penguin represents quality and variety – the very best in publishing today.

For complete information about books available from Penguin – including Puffins, Penguin Classics and Arkana – and how to order them, write to us at the appropriate address below. Please note that for copyright reasons the selection of books varies from country to country.

In the United Kingdom: Please write to *Dept E.P., Penguin Books Ltd, Harmondsworth, Middlesex, UB7 0DA*.

If you have any difficulty in obtaining a title, please send your order with the correct money, plus ten per cent for postage and packaging, to *PO Box No 11, West Drayton, Middlesex*

In the United States: Please write to *Dept BA, Penguin, 299 Murray Hill Parkway, East Rutherford, New Jersey 07073*

In Canada: Please write to *Penguin Books Canada Ltd, 2801 John Street, Markham, Ontario L3R 1B4*

In Australia: Please write to the *Marketing Department, Penguin Books Australia Ltd, P.O. Box 257, Ringwood, Victoria 3134*

In New Zealand: Please write to the *Marketing Department, Penguin Books (NZ) Ltd, Private Bag, Takapuna, Auckland 9*

In India: Please write to *Penguin Overseas Ltd, 706 Eros Apartments, 56 Nehru Place, New Delhi, 110019*

In the Netherlands: Please write to *Penguin Books Nederland B.V., Postbus 195, NL–1380AD Weesp*

In West Germany: Please write to *Penguin Books Ltd, Friedrichstrasse 10–12, D–6000 Frankfurt/Main 1*

In Spain: Please write to *Longman Penguin España, Calle San Nicolas 15, E–28013 Madrid*

In Italy: Please write to *Penguin Italia s.r.l., Via Como 4, I-20096 Pioltello (Milano)*

In France: Please write to *Penguin Books Ltd, 39 Rue de Montmorency, F-75003 Paris*

In Japan: Please write to *Longman Penguin Japan Co Ltd, Yamaguchi Building, 2–12–9 Kanda Jimbocho, Chiyoda-Ku, Tokyo 101*

FOR THE BEST IN PAPERBACKS, LOOK FOR THE

PENGUIN CLASSICS